ROG

Ha

Michelle Dups
xxx
2023

CROW MC #3

BROTHERHOOD & FAMILY BEFORE ALL

By

Michelle Dups

<u>DEDICATIONS</u>

This book is dedicated to all who have felt like they are not enough just as they are.

THANK YOU!

Thank you for taking the time and a chance on me, I hope you enjoy reading my books as much as I enjoy writing them. Books make life a little easier to handle in these strange times.

I write what I like to read. Life is hard enough as it is, so there is little angst in my books. They all have a have happy endings, and strong family vibes with alpha males and strong females.

I am an English author so my American readers will notice a few different words used. As the series commences, I will publish a list in the front of the books. Please feel free to message me with words you are not sure about and I will add them to the list.

I hope you enjoy reading about my Crow MC family and the life they are building for themselves.

List of Characters

CROW MC

ORIGINALS - RETIRED

ALAN CROW (SHEP) m. KATE CROW

Children: KANE (REAPER) AVYANNA (AVY)

ROBERT DAVIES (DOG) m. MAGGIE DAVIES

Children: LIAM (DRACO) MILO (ONYX) IRISH TWINS

BELLAMY (BELLA)

THEO WRIGHT (THOR)

Children: MARCUS (ROGUE) BELLONA (NONI)

JACOB OWENS (GUNNY) (First wife deceased) p. BEVERLY

Children: DRAKE (DRAGON) Adopted: ALEC

JONES - DECEASED

ROMAN - DECEASED

CROW MC

1st GENERATION – ORIGINALS

KANE CROW (REAPER) **PRESIDENT** p.ABBY

Children: SAM, BEN, BREN, ELLIE

LIAM DAVIES (DRACO) **VP**

MILO DAVIES (ONYX) **SGT AT ARMS** p. ANDREA (REA) LAWSON

Children: MILA

MARCUS WRIGHT (ROGUE) **ROAD CAPTAIN** p. JULIA WALKER

DRAKE OWENS (DRAGON) TREASURER

AVYANNA CROW

BELLONA WRIGHT (NONI)

BELLAMY DAVIES (BELLA)

CROW MC

NEW BROTHERS

KEVIN LAWLESS (HAWK) **ENFORCER**

ALAN GOODE (NAVY) **ENFORCER**

SAMUEL ADAMS (BULL) **MEDIC**

PROSPECTS

WILLIAM ADAMS (SKINNY)

TRISTAN JOHNSON (BLAZE)

ANDREW SMITH (BOND)

AMUN JONES (CAIRO)

OTHER CHARACTERS

LEE MASTERS – GYM OWNER

CARLY MASTERS – GRANDDAUGHTER

OLD MAN JENSEN – OWNER OF THE FARM NEXT DOOR TO CROW MANOR

MOLLY JENSEN – GRANDDAUGHTER

WARREN, DEB, DAVID, JULIAN WALKER – JULIA'S BROTHER & FAMILY

BEAU TEMPLE

BOOKER TEMPLE

BRICE TEMPLE

O'SHEA'S

OLD MAN O'SHEA – NONI'S EX-FATHER-IN-LAW

RHETT - NONI'S EX-HUSBAND (IN PRISON)

LIAM

JOHNNY

ADAM

ANDY   YOUNGEST BROTHER SENT TO IRELAND TO FAMILY

MC Owned Businesses

TRICKSTER CAFE

CROW INVESTMENTS

STICKY TRICKY BAKERY

CORVUS PUB

CROW GARAGE

CRAWAN GYM

RAVEN ROOST CAMPSITE – coming soon

List of English Words

Twatwaffle – an idiot – general insult

Yum Yums - It's basically a deep-fried croissant, drenched in icing. They are so delicious.

Trackies/Trackie bottoms – Sweatpants

Trainers – sneakers/running shoes

Wanker – umm self-explanatory I think.

Rogue and Julia's Songs

To Build Something by Malted Milk

Fat Bottomed Girls by Queen

I Can't Help Myself (Sugar Pie, Honey Bunch) by Four Tops

NOTE FROM THE AUTHOR

Hello, my lovely readers!

A little note from me about this book. This book's main female character is slightly larger than what was considered the ideal size for a woman in 2003.

Please note that this book is based in 2003, not long after we came out of the heroin chic phase. Now I am a woman with a Rubenesque frame (my husband's words). However, I was a teenager all through the 90s when being stick thin was all the rage and those of us that weren't had a hard time with teasing, so I get where Julia is coming from.

She has self-esteem issues and is not very confident. However, this book does not only revolve around how she feels and sees herself. It is only a tiny part of the story and how Rogue/Marcus shows her how much he loves every one of her curves.

On a personal note, some of what I raise in this book is a condition I have personal experiences with, as do several women in my family.

I hope I have managed to write about Julia's self-esteem and health issues sympathetically and that you enjoy reading about this couple as much as I loved writing about their journey.

Another note I must add is about the character that fixates on Rogue. Please bear in mind that in no way do our mental health services in the UK work like this, and this is purely fictional. Mental health is taken very seriously here, and everything that can be done to help someone is.

For my last explanation, our school system runs differently from the USA system. In the UK, we have infant, junior, secondary, upper sixth (depending on where you are in the UK) or college.

Children start school (infants) at age 4 or 5, depending on when they are born. Infants is year R, 1 & 2. They then move up to juniors, which is years 3 - 6.

After juniors, they go to secondary school, years 7 – 11, where they do their GCSEs in Year 11. They will finish secondary school at 15/16, depending on when they start.

They then either go to upper sixth (only in some areas of the UK) or go to college to further their education.

After college, they can go to university if they wish or enter the workforce.

Here's to the next instalment of the Crow's MC. I give you Rogue and Julia.

Happy reading!

Michelle

CHAPTER 1

ROGUE

ROSEDALE HOSPICE

FEANNAG VILLAGE

JUNE 2003

It had been six long and, at times, frustrating weeks since I'd first seen Julia at the beach. I'd begun to start feeling a bit like a stalker, but for shit's sake, the woman was hard to pin down.

Women usually fell at my feet. Not Julia, though. She was making me work for it. Although I couldn't say I wasn't enjoying the chase, even if she didn't seem aware that she was being chased.

She intrigued me like nobody I'd ever met. Eventually, I'd had to enlist the help of the women in the family, much to their amusement. I needed help to find out where she was when she was doing errands, so that I could *accidentally* bump into her just to get to talk to her.

While she was always pleasant, she also seemed completely oblivious to my flirting and unsure of my intentions. If it wasn't for her father not doing well, I would have gone gung-ho and swept her off her feet, but I knew she was a little fragile right now and not in the best place for a romance. That was okay. I could go slow.

My predicament was causing great amusement with my brothers, who regularly took the piss out of me. The only ones not giving me a hard time were Reaper and Onyx, but they'd had to go through their own issues to get their women, so they were a little more sympathetic to my plight.

The women in my family outright laughed at me about it, but they did their bit to help me when they could.

My thoughts drifted back to the breakfast at the cafe not so long ago. That had been an interesting morning, to say the least. On the other hand, I didn't care about the drama of having Sam's dad and grandmother turn up to assure us that the ACES were no more. I was more interested in giving the beauty at the table my full attention. However, she seemed totally unaware and treated me much the same as my brothers, much to their amusement.

Finally, I gave up and sat content to just be in the same room as her and watch her instead. But what I noticed didn't make me any happier when she casually put herself down without seeming to realise it about her looks, her weight, or her job. It pissed me off that she couldn't see how fantastic she was, and I vowed if Julia ever gave me the time of day, I would make sure she knew just how beautiful I thought she was.

I'd taken Dragon's advice and started to help with little things like carrying her shopping to the car when I *accidentally* bumped into her at our local supermarket. Then I'd helped her take the crate of books she was taking home to be marked to her car. I happened to be there when I'd been on a school collection run with Abby.

We had slowly graduated from me doing these small things for Julia to me bringing her dinner on the nights she saw her dad at the hospice. She took turns visiting him with her brother, but they called each other every night for updates. She knew it wouldn't be long now, and they had everything in place. I felt for her. I wasn't sure that I'd be as calm if it was my dad.

With me spending so much time with her, she was getting more relaxed in my company. I hadn't done more than rest my hand on her back when I'd walked her to her car or kissed her cheek when I left her place. I loved spending time with her when I could. She was funny, kind and an all-around good person wrapped in one sexy package.

Right then, I was leaning against one of our Range Rovers outside the hospice where her dad was now staying full time, waiting for visiting hours to be over.

Her brother was there with her tonight, as they'd been warned that his time was near. I'd offered to bring her as I'd taken her car to the garage for an MOT and service, and her brother wouldn't be able to pick her up tonight like he usually did.

I didn't mind the wait. It was a beautiful June evening, and the sun was still out at eight o'clock. It was pretty and peaceful under the trees in a balmy eighteen degrees, and the gardens were gorgeous. I could hear trickling water from somewhere, so I assumed there was a fountain further into the garden.

It had just gone eight when Julia came barrelling out of the doors, her face wet with tears, and my heart sank even as it ached for her. I stood up from where I'd been leaning and opened my arms for her. She took the offer and pressed her face into my chest, her body shaking with the force of her sobs as I enclosed her in my arms. I held her tight, pressing my lips to the top of her head.

"I'm so sorry, baby," I whispered.

I looked up as the doors opened again, and her brother walked out. He was a big guy about my height, but wider and more muscular. I knew he worked construction, which was why he'd been late today as he'd been unable to leave the site he was working at on time and had been caught up in traffic.

He looked at his sister in my arms, and I saw the relief on his face, knowing she wasn't alone. Keeping my arms around her, I sent him a chin lift.

"Warren, I'm so sorry for your loss. Is there anything we can do?"

He shook his head and passed a hand over his wet eyes before clearing his throat and replying, "Just look after Julia for me. I have to let my wife and kids know. Other than that, everything is set up. Dad organised it all before he got really sick, and the hospice is helping."

I nodded, and my arms tightened around Julia before I released her to say goodbye to her brother.

She was on autopilot as I helped her into the car and made sure she was buckled in before getting in behind the wheel to take her home. I took her hand, and she held it tight all the way home.

We got to the small house she rented about half an hour later. It was in a pretty good area, and the landlord kept it in good order.

Helping her out of the Range Rover, I walked her to her front door and noticed the envelope taped to her door with her name on it. Taking her house keys from her, I pulled the envelope off and handed it to her before I unlocked the door.

I knew that a few weeks ago, her landlord sent her a letter saying he was considering putting it on the market as he was considering emigrating to Spain. I had a feeling it was a letter of notice informing Julia that he needed the property to be vacated. It couldn't have come on a worse day for her.

Not that she needed to worry. I would make sure she was okay.

I watched as she opened the letter and read it before lifting her face to look at me, her beautiful brown eyes drenched in tears. She handed me the letter to read.

"It's a month's notice to vacate. He's selling." Julia buried her face in her hands and cried. "I don't know what I'm going to do, Marcus. I'll need to rent another place, but I don't have enough money for the three months deposit. I used most of my savings when I took time off work to help with Dad. I can't ask Warren for help. He has a family. I know he'd give me the money for my half of dad's house, but getting a mortgage will take time. Something that I don't have."

Wrapping my arms around her, I held her as she cried, cupping her head where it lay against my chest, her hair silky soft against my palm.

"Shh, Julia. Having somewhere to stay is not something you have to worry about right now. I promise it will be okay. You can move into my wing at the manor with me. It's huge, and I have three bedrooms. Mine is the only one with an ensuite, but there's also a family bathroom is in my wing. You can stay there until you get the money together for a deposit."

She tilted her head on my chest to look at me. "I can't live off you for free, Marcus."

"Of course you can. The manor is paid for, and we all put in money to keep it running, heating and electric, but it's not nearly as much as you'd think. We can discuss you putting money into the pot if you want, but it's not urgent. And it's not something you need to worry about today. Now, how about I run you a bath, and you relax while I get us something to eat? Sounds good?"

"Yeah, it does. Thanks for looking out for me today."

"Anytime, beautiful. Come on, let's get you sorted, fed and into bed. I have a feeling the next few weeks are going to be long and hard for you. So take the time while you have it."

I gently patted her on her bottom and pushed her towards her bedroom. "Go get your PJs, babe. I'll get the bath sorted."

She gave me a small smile before heading to her bedroom.

I headed to the bathroom, got a bath started adding one of the bath bombs she had sitting in a basket on the window sill. Soon the bathroom filled with the scent of jasmine that was all Julia. Hearing a noise, I turned to the door where Julia stood framed in the doorway, her glorious hair held up by a clip, wrapped in a long silky turquoise dressing gown. How this woman didn't realise how gorgeous she was, was beyond me.

Stepping back from the bath, I bowed low, "M'lady, your bath awaits."

In return, I got a slight giggle, which was what I'd been after. Julia stepped back out the door when I approached to leave the bathroom. As I turned to head back to the lounge, I felt a soft hand grip my wrist, and heard a softly uttered, "Marcus."

Turning back towards her, I looked down into her upturned face. She rose on her toes and kissed my cheek softly before saying softly, "Thank you for the last few weeks and for being here with me today. You have made them easier in every way. It means everything."

My throat tightened slightly, clearing it. I pressed a kiss to Julia's forehead before replying, "You're welcome, sweetheart. I'd do just about anything for you."

I left her standing in the bathroom doorway with a look of wonder on her face, and I smiled. I heard the bathroom door close before heading to the kitchen. Opening the fridge, I saw she needed to go grocery shopping but saw some cheese. There was a loaf of bread in the bread bin.

Cheese on toast, it is, then.

There's no better comfort food.

Getting it set out and ready to make on the kitchen counter for when Julia got out of the bath. I pulled out my phone to call Reaper and update him on what had happened. I then called my sister because I knew that as much as we clashed, she would always be there for me and rally the other women to be there for Julia.

CHAPTER 2

JULIA

Relaxing back in the bath that Marcus had run for me, I thought back on today that had been shitty from start to finish. It started with another teacher's complaint in our staff meeting, moaning about me being the only one walking the Crow MC kids to the car park daily. And if the MC were worried about security, then surely it should be all the teachers having a go on a roster. I knew what the issue was with this particular teacher. She'd had her eye on the MC men from day one. And I knew she had the hots for Marcus.

I hadn't had to say anything as the head teacher had been told in no uncertain terms that the children trusted only me, as I was the only one that had done anything when they were struggling.

The head had made it clear to all staff members that I was the only one to take the children out to the car park and that they were aware that if I wasn't available, they would wait in the office to be collected.

She'd shut up after that, and I'd gone about my day, but I'd had to listen to snide remarks from her throughout the day and in the staff room. I'd managed to block most of it out, but I couldn't ignore that her comments about my weight had hurt. She was pretty clever, or maybe sneaky was a better way of thinking about it in making sure no one was around when she made her comments.

I knew it would only escalate after Marcus had picked me up to take me to see my dad when he and Abby had arrived to pick up the children. It would escalate because it's the type of woman Elizabeth Gaines was, and she'd made it pretty clear to all in the teachers' lounge in the last few weeks that she had a thing for Marcus.

I'd kept my mouth shut, as I knew there was no way any of the MC men would go for someone as loud and brash as her. While their women were no pushovers, they weren't rude or unkind.

Adjusting the rolled-up towel behind my head, I released a sigh and felt my body relax further in the warmth of the bath. The familiar smell of my bath salts added to the sense of comfort.

While Warren and I had known our dad's time was near and we were prepared, it had still hit me hard when he'd drawn his last breath that evening. All I could think of was getting to Marcus, who was waiting for me in the car park.

I smiled a little as my thoughts drifted to our first meeting at the beach. I hadn't known what to think of Marcus and thought he was just after a good time with a big girl. Easy pickings, as I'd been by a previous man.

I mean, he was gorgeous, tall and muscular with auburn hair and eyes so dark blue they looked navy. What would a guy that looked like him want with a woman like me? I was closer in age to thirty than twenty. I was of average height and a size eighteen on a good day, with an arse that jiggled when I walked. I had dimples on my knees, for Christ's sake.

I liked to think I was a good person with a good sense of humour. Thanks to genetics, I knew I had a pretty face and good skin. Still, genetics had also screwed me when it came to hormones. I ended up with endometriosis and polycystic ovary syndrome at the same time as my mum did. I'd had to make a tough decision in my late twenties when my pain had gotten so bad that I'd opted to have a full hysterectomy, which threw me into early menopause. I'd not been in a good place for a few years, but with lots of therapy, great doctors, my school kids, and my family, I'd felt more like my old self in the last eighteen months.

Marcus and I started bumping into each other regularly after breakfast at the cafe a few weeks ago. At first, I couldn't understand why we kept bumping into each other when I'd never seen him out and about before. And then he somehow wangled an invitation to my house and brought supper with him.

I thought he was just being friendly and spending time with him was no hardship. I saw a side of him that he didn't show when he was out with this family.

However, it seemed that I was a bit slow on the uptake, and it was his sister who eventually let the cat out of the bag last Saturday when I joined them for lunch at the cafe.

I'd mentioned that Marcus had been over for supper twice last week, and I'd seen the looks they'd exchanged and the grins.

Narrowing my eyes, I wondered what I was missing and if this was where they started making fun of me? I hadn't thought they were the type of women that would be cruel, but I'd also learned the hard way that people weren't always to be trusted.

"What's going on?" I questioned.

Noni grinned and answered, "We were just wondering how long you would make Rogue work for some attention. We've all been taking the piss out of him that his charm isn't working this time."

I frowned, confused at her comment. "I don't understand what you mean."

Noni looked at me, surprised, "You mean you don't know how hot my brother is for you? I thought you were just making out that you were oblivious, not that you actually were."

I'd been both hurt and angry that they would think I would ever treat someone like that, and I'd let them know. Usually, I would have just left and not bothered to answer their calls or made excuses as to why I couldn't meet up if they ever asked me to meet again. I didn't like confrontation, but I wouldn't let this go. Marcus didn't deserve to be teased about something that wasn't his fault.

"Noni, I'm hurt and a little pissed that you would think I'd ever treat someone like that. First, I would never want to make someone feel like they weren't worth my while. Secondly, your brother has been nothing but the utmost gentleman to me when we spend time together. He's funny, sweet and not at all what I expected. That you have all been giving him a hard time doesn't sit well with me, and I'm beginning to reconsider this friendship," I said, throwing my serviette on my plate and going to stand up.

Avy's hand on my arm stopped me, "You're right, Julia. We should have realised that you didn't know he was interested. You aren't the type to string a man along. It's just it's been refreshing watching him have to work for attention for a change. Usually, women just fall at his feet. Not just his feet, I admit. All of them have no trouble getting women. Please, don't leave. We love having you as part of our circle, and if Rogue finds out we hurt you, he will get seriously pissed at us."

I sat back down, still not sure whether I wanted to continue my friendship with them. However, I did listen, and there was some amusement as they told me how he'd recruited all of them to keep him informed on what I was doing.

I'd wondered why I'd kept getting texts from all the women asking what I was up to every morning. When they knew some of my schedules, he'd arrange it so he would *bump* into me. It made my heart flutter a little that he would put so much work into spending time with me. I was still a little hesitant, though. I mean, he could have anybody, and he wanted me. I didn't understand it.

"Okay, thanks for telling me and making me understand where he's coming from. I'm still a little confused, though. I mean, why me, of all people, when he could have anyone?"

Rea snorted and said, "Girl, because you're gorgeous, have an awesome personality, and are kind to boot. You're just his type. And trust me, I've known that man since I was fourteen. Both he and Dragon prefer women that will not break when they take them to bed."

I felt my face flush at Rea's comment. I couldn't deny I'd fantasised about Marcus and how he'd be in bed, but I never thought it would be an actual possibility. My B.O.B. had gotten a lot of workouts in the last few weeks.

Turning to Noni, Rea said, "You may want to close your ears if you don't want to know about your brother's sex life."

Noni grumbled but put her fingers in her ears, looking a little green at the thought of knowing what Marcus liked in bed, though I was intrigued.

I sniggered at her and laughed out loud when Noni stuck her tongue out at me before turning my attention back to Rea, who continued. "As I said, I've known them a long time, and Dragon and Rogue have always preferred women with fuller figures. From conversations I've overheard, both men like it a little rough in bed. Oh, don't get me wrong, they don't hurt their bed partners, but they're big guys, Julia. Bigger than most. They've always said that when they are with smaller women, they are always scared of hurting them and end up not enjoying the whole experience. I also think it has something to do with who taught them about sex, but that's another story. Petite, skinny women have never got their motors running for as long as I've known them.

"Plus, have a look around at the women in this family. None of us is under a size twelve. Not all men want a size six. If that were the case, we'd all be single. Yes, I get you're bigger than what society deems acceptable, but you're not unhealthy. I've seen your records. I know you struggle with your weight, but you do everything right, exercise, eat healthily, and don't smoke or drink excessively. You are gorgeous, and only you don't see that."

My eyes filled with tears as I looked around the table, and it was as if blinkers had fallen off my eyes. The smallest, at probably a size twelve, were Rea and Avy, but they were also the smallest in stature. Noni and Bev were both probably a size sixteen. I wasn't sure because I didn't judge people on their size, just on how they were as people. It hit me then that I judged myself in a way I didn't judge others.

"Ah," Bev smiled at me warmly and squeezed my hand. "She gets it."

I took the serviette that Abby handed me and wiped my eyes.

"So, he really likes me, huh? He's not just looking to pass the time with a hit and quit it?"

"Babe, please, the man is hot for you. Can you put him out of his misery and throw the man a bone," Abby smirked at me.

I'd left them that day feeling lighter than I'd felt in a long time and had planned on making my interest known to Marcus now that I realised he did actually find me attractive and wasn't just a nice guy making my life easier during a difficult time.

Unfortunately, my dad's health started to decline even further around the same time, and I'd been focused on him and helping my brother. Marcus had been in the background, always willing to help and support. It had made everything easier, and then this evening, when Dad had passed away, through my tears and grief, my one thought was that I just needed to get through this and to Marcus, who was waiting for me outside. I knew I would be okay once I was in his arms.

I'd been right. I felt better as soon as Marcus' arms enclosed me. Then to come home to the tenancy letter had thrown me again.

My memories were broken by a knock on the door.

"Babe, are you okay?" Marcus called out, sounding concerned.

I realised the water had grown cold while I was wool-gathering. I must have been here a while.

"I'm fine, honey, just getting out now," I answered without thinking.

There was an intake of breath at my endearment before he stated softly through the door, "Okay, sweetheart, I'm just starting to make cheese on toast. Take your time."

I made short work of rinsing off and getting out of the bath, moisturising my whole body. I got dressed in a pair of shorts and a t-shirt before adding a thin hoodie. Even if the evenings were warmer, there was still a bit of a nip in the air.

Leaving the bathroom, I joined Marcus in the kitchen, where he put the cheese on toast on plates. My mouth watered at the smell. There was nothing quite like comfort food.

He nodded at the small table I had in the kitchen, handing me my phone. Then, he added, "Your phone has been going crazy."

Opening it up, I saw all the messages. Every single one was from a member of his family or from the MC, letting me know they were thinking of me and to let them know if there was anything they could do for me.

I blinked my eyes rapidly to stop the tears from falling. "They are all from your family and the MC," I told him.

He nodded, not looking surprised. I guessed he must have told them.

"You're not alone, baby. You and Warren just need to tell us what we can do to make this easier for you. Now, eat up and then get into bed. I'll clean up and lock up before I leave."

I bit my lip and looked at him under my lashes before saying, "You could stay the night if you want."

His blue eyes contemplated me from under raised brows before he smiled and said, "There's nothing I'd like more."

I nodded with a smile and went back to my food.

While my day had started off shit and only worsened as the day proceeded. With Dad being terminal for so long, Warren and I'd made peace with his death long ago, even though it had been hard to watch him take his last breath. In a way, it had been a relief. He was no longer in pain and was hopefully at peace with my mum.

It felt right letting Marcus know that I wanted him here with me. My dad wouldn't have wanted us to wait. Life was short, and I needed to grab on with both hands and start living my life.

CHAPTER 3

ROGUE

To say I was surprised at Julia's offer to stay the night was an understatement, but I wouldn't look a gift horse in the mouth. I knew there had been some sort of disagreement between the women last weekend, as Noni had admitted she'd hurt Julia's feelings. Still, they'd settled their differences, and it was all sorted.

I hadn't been happy to hear that they'd hurt her, but I didn't say anything as she'd seemed fine when I'd next seen her.

I finished my food and watched as she picked at hers, but I didn't remark on it as she'd eaten most of it. Her eyelids had drooped for the last few minutes, and she'd shaken herself awake a few times. The woman was bloody stubborn, that's for sure. She'd sit there exhausted until I said something, then would try to fight me about going to bed.

"Babe, head to bed. You're exhausted."

Her head snapped up, and her eyes opened wide. "No, I'm fine. Let me clean up as you cooked."

Julia started to collect our plates and went to stand.

With a hand on her wrist, I stopped her and said softly, "Beautiful, I've got this. Head to bed. I'll lock up and be in shortly."

She bit her lip and looked at me from under her lashes before nodding, "Okay, thank you."

I let her go and watched as she left the kitchen, her arse jiggling a little as she walked, and my cock got hard watching her walk away. I couldn't wait to have her on her knees so I could watch those globes jiggling as I pounded into her.

I let out a low moan as I pressed down hard on my cock for some relief that I knew wouldn't be coming for a while. I couldn't wait to get Julia into bed, show her how much I loved her body, and have her learn to love herself as much as I did. Not tonight, though. Tonight, I'd hold her and make sure she knew she wasn't alone.

Making quick work of cleaning up, I walked around the house, making sure it was locked up for the night before I put another call into Reaper.

While the ACES were no more, he still liked us to check in with him. Reaper was like a fucking mother hen who wanted all her chicks in with her at night. I knew if I didn't call, he'd either call me or send a couple of brothers to check on me. Once we were in bed, I didn't want anyone bothering us.

Holding the phone to my ear, I waited as it rang, and he finally answered, "You got Reaper."

From the noise in the background, I assumed he was at the pub with Avy.

"Hey Reap, letting you know I'm staying at Julia's tonight."

"Okay, brother. Is she doing okay?"

"Seems to be. She's a bit tearful, but he was sick and in pain for a long time. Warren and Julia have been expecting this for a while, and in a way, I think it's a relief for them that he's not in pain anymore. She's tough, and I'll make sure she's okay."

"Good thing Rogue. Give us a shout if they need anything. Avy says to let her know if they want to use the VIP room for a wake, and Aunt Maggie has said she will cater for them at no charge."

My throat tightened at the generosity of my family, clearing it before I spoke again. "Thanks, man, and thank Aunt Maggie. I'll let Julia and Warren know. Night Reap."

I got a "Night, brother." before he hung up the phone.

Heading towards the hall, I stopped at the bathroom and had a quick shower before walking to the bedroom. She'd left a bedside light on for me. My attention was taken by the woman fast asleep in the bed. Stepping closer, I noticed she had tears drying on her cheeks, but otherwise, her face was relaxed. She had a sheet pulled up over her to her waist, her shoulders bare, but I could see the thin strap of her Cami showing, the duvet was pushed to the bottom of the bed.

Walking around the bed, I pulled the sheet back, dropped my towel and climbed in bare-arsed naked and hoped she'd not freak because there was no way I could sleep with clothes on, and I wasn't going to put my dirty boxers back on.

Switching off the lamp, I turned and put my arm over her waist, pulling her tight into me, burying my face in her dark hair and inhaling her scent. I relaxed. Finally, she was in my arms, and all was right with my world, or it would be once I had her in my wing back at the manor.

CHAPTER 4

JULIA

It had been three weeks since my dad passed away. Today was the day of the funeral. Marcus's family had stepped up in a big way and arranged a wake, and catered all the food in the VIP room at the pub.

Neither Warren nor I had ever had this type of support, and it took a while for us to get used to it. We'd been adopted into the family like it was nothing, and I'd learned that being part of the Crow MC family was wonderful.

I'd not been on my own once in the last three weeks. Rogue had slept every night with me, and if he had to be away, he arranged for one of his family to stay or had me go to the manor. I'd often slept in his wing at Crow Manor and was quickly becoming used to being there. With the number of people around, I didn't have the time to wallow, as something was always happening. I only had to disappear to Marcus' wing if I wanted peace and quiet.

Marcus and I hadn't moved past just sleeping together, and he seemed content to hold me and not push for anything more. It had been the best I'd slept in years. I guessed he was waiting for me to make a move. I was gathering up my courage, but first, I needed to get past today before we could start on our new lives.

It had been a beautiful service in a local church that Dad had attended. Neither Warren nor I had to do much, as Dad sorted it when he got sick. I was grateful it had all moved along smoothly, and he was now buried next to mum.

I stood next to Warren, my arm tucked into his as we stood next to our parents' graves, paying our last respects. Everyone else had left for the pub, including Warren's wife Deb, who'd said she would go help but not before giving me a hug. I was eternally grateful that Warren had married a woman that I liked.

We were close siblings. There were only eleven months between us, and we had grown up much like twins. We'd done most things together growing up. He was my best friend.

Letting go of his arm, I leant forward and placed the daisy I'd been holding that I'd taken from the flowers on Dad's coffin and placed it on mum's gravestone.

Pressing a kiss to my palm, I laid it on the stone. "Love you, Mum. I hope you are together again," I said softly before standing back up.

Warren took my arm and steadied me when I wobbled in my heels where they'd got stuck in the grass.

"Just you and me now, sis," he said sadly before turning to me and wiping his eyes.

Smiling sadly, I took the tissue that Marcus had handed me in church and gently wiped my brother's face.

"No, bub, it's you, me, Deb, your boys and the Crow MC," I replied.

He chuffed out a laugh and took the tissue I handed him. "Yeah, who would have thought? I haven't asked, but what's happening with you and Rogue?"

"Honestly, I'm still not sure. According to his sister, he has a thing for me, but I can't understand why. He could have anyone, Warren. Why me? My heart tells me to go for it, but I'm having trouble with my head," I muttered, frustrated with myself.

Warren put his arm around me, and we started the walk back to the car park.

"I hate that you can't see yourself like the rest of us do, Jules. You're gorgeous and have a great personality, so what if you don't reach societal norms? They are overrated, anyway. And I never thought I'd say this about my sister but I don't want to know what that man thinks when he looks at you like you're the last cupcake on the plate, and he needs to have it."

I giggled at the faint disgust in his voice.

"He's asked me to move into his wing at the manor until I find somewhere else to rent," I told Warren.

Warren stopped walking and turned me towards him, hands firm on my shoulders, before saying seriously, "Are you okay with that? We can make room for you at ours. We can double up the boys until we get a mortgage sorted out, and I can pay you out your half of the house."

I smile at the concern in his voice, "It's fine, bub, I guess it will give us time to see where this is going, and I've mostly been staying over there for the last few weeks, anyway. Plus, unless I imagined it, I'm sure I saw Deb hiding a little bump under that throw she had on," I retorted with a smile.

Warren's ears turned red at the tips as we continued walking. "Yeah," he answered gruffly. "It was an unexpected but not unwelcome surprise. Shit, sis, there's an eight-year age gap between this one and our youngest. We thought we were done. Dad was thrilled when I told him. I thought he needed to know before he passed."

I laughed. This was just the news we needed on a day like today.

"I bet he was. He loved your boys. Maybe this time, it will be a girl that I get to spoil."

He grinned at the thought, "Maybe. We'll find out next week."

"Good, I want a phone call before you even leave the hospital car park," I informed him, smiling. "Now come on, I see Marcus waiting for us, and I need to go and congratulate the new mama."

We picked up our pace, and I smiled when I felt a flutter low in my belly as I saw Marcus patiently waiting, leaning against the door of the Range Rover he'd driven today. He'd taken his jacket off, undone his tie so that it was lying loose around his neck and rolled his dark blue shirt sleeves up to his elbows, showing off his tattoos. He must have been running his hand through his hair because it was ruffled up.

The man was a helluva sexy package. And he wanted to be mine. Who was I to deny him? Or me?

Letting go of my brother's arm, I walked with purpose up to Marcus, rose on my toes, and kissed his lips.

I sank back on my heels and opened my eyes, and I watched as his eyes flared in surprise before he pressed his lips to mine in another hard kiss.

He lifted his head and said with a growl, "Not sure what brought that on, but I can't say I'm unhappy about it." Then he grinned and said, "I don't know what you and Warren were discussing, but I'm guessing you've come to a decision. For now, let's get you to the pub and get this day done. Yeah?"

"Yeah," I agreed with a smile and got in the car. Hearing the back door open, I turned and saw Warren getting in. He looked up and winked at me. "Dad would be thrilled for you, Jules."

I smiled and turned to look out the window and thought, yes, he would be. It's all he ever wanted was for me to find someone who loved me as much as he'd loved our mum.

CHAPTER 5

ROGUE

I'd stood watching as everyone else had left the cemetery and left Julia and Warren to say goodbye to their dad in peace.

She'd leant and placed a flower on what could only be their mother's grave, and my heart had hurt when I saw her kiss her palm and lay it on the gravestone.

They'd said their goodbyes, and I'd seen how Julia comforted her brother, showing the strength I knew she had in her. Not that she seemed to realise how strong she was.

They'd turned and strolled back to the car park, holding a serious conversation. I wondered what it was about before they continued on.

Warren had said something to her before they got to the car, and I'd seen on her face when she came to a decision and had hotfooted it my way, taking me by surprise when she'd kissed me. Not looking a gift horse in the mouth, I'd returned it.

I'd caught the wink her brother had given her as he got in the car, but hadn't said anything. She'd seemed happy enough, so I left it. There would be plenty of time for us to go forward with our lives, but today wasn't it.

All in all, considering what this day was about, it had gone well. There had been friends of her parents at the wake reminiscing about their younger days. Julia had made sure she went around everyone, thanking them for coming. Three hours later, I could see the exhaustion on her face. I stepped in, had her sit down, and got her a plate of food.

"They can come to you, babe, but you need to eat and drink something," I informed her.

She'd looked at me with relief and smiled her dimpled smile at me, replying, "Thanks, honey."

Tucking a piece of hair that had come out of her plait behind her ear, "Don't move from here until you've eaten all that," I ordered. "What do you want to drink?"

"Just water, please."

I nodded and asked her sister-in-law, Deb, who'd sat down next to Julia, "What about you, Deb?"

"I'm good, thanks, Rogue. Warren is getting me some food and drink."

Nodding, I headed to the bar to get a bottle of water, passing Warren on the way, who stopped me as I went to walk past him.

"Rogue."

"Hey, Warren, do you need anything?"

He shook his head. "No, I just wanted to say thanks for all you've done for Julia in the last few weeks. And if you ever need anything, you only have to ask."

Tilting my head and looking him in the eye, I decided to lay some things out. It probably wasn't the time or place, but I didn't give a fuck. He needed to know I was serious about his sister.

"Warren, nothing I do for Julia is too much. I get she's not sure yet, but I'm telling you now that your sister is it for me. I'll go slow until it sinks in with her. When the time is right, I'll come to you and ask but know that I plan to marry her as soon as I think she's ready. First, though, I have to get her to see herself the way I see her."

"Okay," he acquiesced. "Thanks for letting me know, although I kind of already figured that was where it was heading. Let me know when you are moving her into your wing, and I'll make sure I'm there to help," he grinned at my surprised look. "Yep, she made a decision. Welcome to the family," he chuckled as he walked towards his sister and wife.

Shaking my head in bemusement, I headed to the bar and asked Avy for a bottle of water and a coke.

Feeling a familiar hand clasp my shoulder hard, I wasn't surprised when I heard my dad's voice ask, "What's up, son? You look confused."

Turning my head to look at him where he was leaning against the bar next to me, I replied, "Not confused, more like bemused."

He snorted a laugh, "Fuck, son, bemused, really? You sleep with a dictionary last night?"

I laughed aloud, "Fuck off, old man. You make it sound like I'm not educated. No, just that Julia told Warren she'd move in with me."

My dad beamed a happy grin at me, "That's fantastic news, Rogue. I'm happy for you. She has made you work for it, but I like her for you. She's a good woman from what I've seen, and she's loyal, doesn't take shit either and can stand up for herself when needed. Your sister told me what happened at the cafe, she felt bad about it. But she said that Julia stuck up for you and wouldn't have anyone bad mouth you or give you a hard time, including your brothers.

"I know for a fact that she went to every brother in the MC and told them to lay off you. Didn't you wonder why they hadn't been giving you a hard time the last couple of weeks?"

Shaking my head, I was amazed that she'd done that. I knew she hated confrontation of any kind, "No, I just figured it was because of the funeral and me not being at home much that they'd stopped. She really went to all the brothers?"

"She did," Gunny said, nodding from where he'd been standing next to dad. "Went up in everyone's estimation. Good woman, I suggest you lock her down soon as possible."

"Working on it, Gunny," I agreed, taking the drinks from Avy. "Thanks, Avy."

"No problem, Rogue. Tell Julia I'll catch up with her later, but if she needs anything, just ask."

"Will do, Avs, thanks," I confirmed, kissing her cheek in thanks.

Giving my dad and Gunny a chin tilt, I headed back to the woman who held my heart, feeling happier than I had in a long while, knowing she would soon be under the same roof as me.

CHAPTER 6

JULIA

It was moving weekend. I'd spent the week after Dad's funeral at work or at my rental packing up and deciding what I no longer needed so I could give it to charity. Rogue had been with me every step of the way, and when he wasn't helping out at the garage or one of the other businesses the MC owned, he was here helping me.

We still hadn't had sex, and I'd started wondering why. He seemed content to hold, cuddle and kiss me long and hard but nothing more, not even a quick grope. Nada, nothing! I'd never in all my life been so sexually frustrated.

I finally cracked and asked him what was happening last night when we were lying in bed.

It was late. We'd snuggled into bed after showers. The man was hot naked, and he was not shy about it. He had firm muscled legs and thighs and a broad, muscular chest that was spattered with a little red hair and freckles. My eyes loved to travel down to that delicious V usually showcased by the towel he wore before he got into bed. He always switched the light off just before he dropped the towel and got into bed. He found it hilarious when I grumbled. I loved that he slept naked, tight against me and wished I was brave enough to lose my pyjamas, but I wasn't there yet.

Right then, I had my head pillowed on his chest with an arm over his chest and a leg thrown over his hips. He ran his hand up and down my back, sometimes slowing to massage my lower back, making me melt into him.

"Rogue?"

"Mmm," he rumbled.

"Why haven't we had sex?"

The hand on my back stilled, and his body stiffened before he reached over and turned the bedside lamp on. I bit my lip, wondering if he was angry at my question, but his face was soft when he turned back to me.

Pushing me to lie back, he fitted his body over mine. I opened my legs so I could cradle his body between them. Feeling the hardness of his cock pressing against the seam of my pyjama shorts. Letting me know he wasn't unaffected by our cuddling in bed.

His hands framed my face as he pushed my hair back from my face. He pressed a soft kiss to the corner of my mouth before moving to my ear, where he nipped at the lobe, making me jump and whimper.

"Because beautiful, when we make love, I want all your attention to be focused on us. Not grieving or packing and moving. You are worth the wait, and don't ever think I don't want you."
He paused as he thrust his hard cock against me. I tilted my hips, hoping for more

friction. Instead, he continued slowly pressing kisses down my throat to my chest. "Now, if you tell me that you are horny and would like a little relief, baby, I'd be more than happy to help you with that."

I gasped as he sucked hard on my nipple through my cami. The hot wetness of his mouth on the silk made my clit start to throb, and I could feel myself getting wet. Whimpering low in my throat, I rocked my hips against his as he moved his attention to my other breast.

Then he stopped. I growled in frustration and looked at him to find him grinning at me. I frowned at him and rocked my hips again, needing more pressure. He put a hand on my hip, holding me still.

He shook his head, "Uh, uh. You want me to make you come. You have to ask for it."

I bit my lip, unsure. I'd have to get naked, and the light was on.

"Can we switch the light off?"

His eyes softened before he shook his head, "No, beautiful, I want to see you when you come. To me, you are gorgeous. There is nothing you need to hide from me."

I searched his eyes to see if he was lying, but all I saw was sincerity, making a decision, helped by the fact that I was horny as hell. I nodded.

"Okay." I breathed out and asked for what I needed. "Please make me come." I could feel the blush at having to ask, spreading from my chest up my face.

"My pleasure, baby," Marcus smiled, helping me sit up and pulling my cami off over my head. He bit his lip seductively as he watched my breasts bounce as he removed it. He groaned low in his throat and licked his lips, his eyes intent on me. Pushing me back on the bed, he again focused his attention on my breasts, and before long, I was squirming, wanting, needing. I hadn't realised they were so sensitive. He didn't disappoint. There wasn't an inch of me that wasn't covered in kisses and small nips. I was so wet I was dripping, but he kept ignoring the part of me that needed me most. I broke, grabbed his hand and pushed it down my pyjama shorts.

"I was getting there," he rumbled.

"Not fast enough," I muttered, gasping as his fingers slowly pushed into me.

"Fuck, baby. You're soaked," he growled before pulling his fingers from me. I let out a little wail of frustration. "Shh, sweetheart, I'll give you what you need. Let's get rid of these," he said, pulling my shorts off and throwing them on the floor.

He settled between my legs and ran his fingers through my wetness. "So pretty, baby, and all for me," he pressed a finger and then another into me. I gasped at the fullness. Pumping his fingers a few times, he made a come-hither gesture, and I rocked my hips. Pulling his fingers out, I watched as he sucked my wetness off them with a look of bliss on his face,

"Delicious," he rumbled.

Slowly he pushed his fingers back into my folds before disappearing between my raised legs. His fingers not letting up as his lips found my clit and sucked it deep into his mouth. I just about levitated off the bed. It was so good. I could feel my orgasm approaching, my toes tingling, and my thighs shaking. Pressing my hands against the headboard, I ground my pussy against his face as he flattened his tongue and pressed hard against me before sucking my clit hard again, and I was done for. I came hard, tears in my eyes, my breath sawing in and out of my chest as my hips stilled. I'd never felt like this before. As I came down, I fully expected Marcus to fuck me, but instead, I found him kneeling between my raised knees, watching me with a slight smile on his face, his eyes happy, and his hand gripping his rock-hard cock slowly moving up and down.

"Your turn," I said softly, reaching for him.

He got off the end of the bed, walked around and knelt on the bed next to me, taking my hand. He folded my fingers around his hard cock and then enclosed it with his as he showed me how he liked it and how to move my hand. It was the hottest thing I'd ever seen. The two of us jacking him off, I was getting turned on again, and my free hand drifted to my clit. Marcus watched as I circled my fingers around it, raising my knees to get better access. He swapped the hand on his cock to his left and added the fingers of his right hand to mine, circling my clit. It was the hottest thing I'd ever done. His fingers left mine to work my clit, and he thrust his fingers into my still-wet pussy, triggering another orgasm.

"Oh my god," I wailed as I came just as I felt warm jets of cum hit my stomach.

Marcus had his head thrown back, the tendons in his neck taught as he finished on me. He pulled his fingers out of me and sucked them off, his face flushed and eyes drowsy. He bent and kissed me long and hard. It was then I realised that not once during what we'd just done had I thought about my round stomach, my squishy thighs or my dimpled knees. He'd totally blown my mind.

He pressed soft kisses down my throat and to my breast, his hands running up and down my body. I was so relaxed I melted into the bed.

"Well, that escalated. Especially after me saying we'd wait," he ground out hoarsely against my chest. I ran my fingers through his hair and chuffed out a laugh at his words.

"Feeling better, beautiful?"

"Yeah," I nodded and smiled at him.

"Good, stay there, and I'll get something to clean you up," he replied with a small sated smile.

Getting off the bed, he headed to the bathroom, his muscles flexing in his arse as he walked away. I let out a happy sigh at the view and enjoyed it even more when he walked back in, still naked. Not sure which view I preferred, the front or the back.

He chuckled when I licked my lips.

"Babe, we need to sleep," he rumbled as he swiped a warm washcloth between my legs, making me blush even more.

I'd never had anyone do this for me. Then, folding the washcloth, he used it to clean his cum from my body. I was a little disappointed. I liked wearing him.

He threw the cloth on top of his towel and climbed back into bed. I went to get up to get my PJs.

He stopped me by pulling me towards him and curling himself around me. "Where are you going?"

"To get my PJs," I replied.

He shook his head, "Uh, uh, nope, no more PJ's in bed. Now that I've felt your skin against me, I don't want anything in between us."

"Marcus, I've never slept naked," I stammered slightly, but I did like the feel of his skin against mine.

"Don't worry, beautiful, you'll get used to it," he reassured me, pulling me tighter against him. "Sleep, love. Busy day tomorrow."

I settled against him, throwing a leg over his hips and feeling his cock against my thigh. I grinned a little. Yeah, I could see the advantages of sleeping naked, I thought as sleep claimed me.

CHAPTER 7

ROGUE

The last of Julia's boxes had been brought up to my wing. We'd made short work of it with all of us and the kids pitching in. Warren had come to help, but Julia had sent him home as Deb, his wife, wasn't feeling well.

For once, I was content. The constant need and restlessness to be on the move had disappeared over the last month. I knew I would still travel, but now I looked forward to travelling with someone.

I left the spare room where we'd piled most of Julia's boxes for her to go through and find a place for her things. She still thought she'd be moving to a rental, but now that I had her in my room in my house, I was going to work my arse off to keep her there.

Wandering back to my bedroom, I saw my woman unpacking her suitcases and hanging clothing in my wardrobe. I'd cleaned out and made space for her weeks ago. It felt right seeing our things hanging next to each other.

Walking up behind her, I wrapped my arms around her waist and pulled her tight to me, pressing a kiss to her neck.

"Why do you always smell so good," I muttered, running my nose up her neck before turning her in my arms.

She smiled up at me, the dimples in her cheeks deepening with her smile, her brown eyes sparkling and stress-free.

"Only you think I smell good, Marcus. I can't imagine that I do, especially after sweating and moving everything today," she laughed, hugging me tight.

"Nobody else better get close enough to be able to smell you," I growled possessively, lowering my mouth to hers and running my tongue along the seam of her lips, nudging them open before deepening the kiss. I ran my hands down her back to her hips and grabbed a handful of her rear, pulling her tight against me. My cock hardened, and I rubbed it against her for some relief. She gasped slightly and rocked against me. We were so lost in each other that we didn't hear them traipsing up the stairs until Abby called out.

"Whoops, sorry," Abby said from the doorway. Rea stood next to her.

I lifted my head and glared with narrowed eyes at the open doorway where my brother's women were framed.

"Yeah, no. Abby may be sorry, but I'm not," Rea responded with a smirk. "Payback's a bitch, Rogue. I'm sorry for the clam jam Jules, but Rogue deserves the cock block."

Julia snorted a laugh as she buried her head against my chest.

"What do you two want?" I muttered.

"Hey, don't get pissy with us. You should have closed the door if you were going to get your freak on. It could have been one of the kids," Abby growled, mamma bear out in full force.

I sighed, knowing she was right. The kids had the freedom to roam where they wanted.

"You're right, Abs, sorry. What can we do for you, ladies?"

"That's better," she snipped, then ruined it with a happy smile, clapping her hands. "The boys have started the barbecue, and we have margaritas, and woo woos ready. Jules, hurry up and get your arse downstairs. Unpacking can wait. We've even persuaded Molly to come over."

"Does Draco know?" I inquired with a slight grin letting go of Julia so she could finish what she'd been doing.

"Nope, and we're not telling him. Those two are going to be the comedic relief for the evening," Avy said, popping up from behind the two women in the doorway. "What's taking you guys so long? The ice is melting and watering down the cocktails."

"I'm coming, I'm coming," Julia shouted from the bathroom, where she'd disappeared with the last small bag that had been on our bed.

"You're not, but you would have been if this lot hadn't interrupted us," I shouted back at her, hearing a gasp from the bathroom.

The three in the door started cackling like hyenas at my words. Julia came out of the bathroom swinging a towel at me, her face flushed with embarrassment.

"I can't believe you said that," she burst out as she flicked the towel at me, making me laugh and jumped over the bed running for the doorway to get away. The three women there tried to keep me from getting out. I made it through them, but not before Julia got me good with the towel, she was evil, and I'd forgotten how much getting flicked by a towel hurt.

I knew she wasn't pissed at me, though, because when I caught her eyes over the heads of Avy, Rea, and Abby, she was laughing just as much as them.

Blowing her a kiss, I called out, "See you at the clubhouse, beautiful." Turning, I headed downstairs and out towards the clubhouse, where I could smell the coal from the barbecues.

As I walked over, I knew I had a stupid grin on my face. I couldn't help it. Julia made me happy. It didn't go unnoticed by my brothers, who all wanted to know what I was grinning about. Not that I'd say anything. I figured the women would let them know sooner or later.

For now, a beer, burning some meat and spending time with my brothers sounded like a good plan.

CHAPTER 8

JULIA

It was late. The barbecue was a memory from the afternoon. Some of the oldies had headed up to the house earlier with the kids to watch a movie and have a snack before bed. It left the second generation free to have a good night and the grandparents' time with their grandchildren.

We girls were feeling the cocktails that Avy had kept us supplied with. I was having a great time. The fire pit behind the clubhouse was burning, taking off the chill of the evening. We were sitting around chatting. Marcus was sitting on the patio floor, leaning back, his head resting against my legs. I ran my fingers through his hair as he chatted with Dragon, sitting next to us. Every time I stopped, he'd rub his cheek against my leg until I started again. It made me smile, but I happily continued. I was beginning to understand these men were totally different from what I was used to. They revered the women in their lives. I'd seen it with Maggie and Kate. Then again, how they treated Noni, Avy, and Bella and how they showed the boys how to treat women and Bren and Ella on how they should expect to be treated. They were a family, and they would do anything for each other. It didn't matter if the person were blood or not.

I was surprised when I was told I would be invited to the first part of their Church meetings and could stay for the second part if I wished.

After finding out what the second part of Church entailed, I declined. Nope. I'd happily bury my head in the sand and let the guys keep us safe.

To my right, I was half listening to a conversation between Marcus and Dragon. They were discussing a bike that was for sale that they wanted to see. It needed work, but they figured it would do for one of the boys to fix it up.

I'd been having my own conversation with the girls about Elizabeth Gaines, the jealous bitch at the school that had been making my life miserable for the last two weeks that I'd been back. I think it was the cocktails that made me brave enough, or it could be I was sick of the snide remarks and her general bitchiness. Either way, I was opening up to the women and telling them how I'd taken to not bothering to venture into the teachers' lounge, instead spending time in my classroom or out on the field with whoever was on duty.

A few of the other teachers had noticed her behaviour, and I'd been told several times to report it to the head teacher and the education department at the local council.

I'd been hoping it would blow over, but it hadn't. I'd started keeping a diary and recording her when I could. I'd also arranged a meeting with the head teacher on Monday. I told them all this.

"What kind of shit is she saying?" Noni demanded angrily.

"Stuff you really don't want to know about," I retorted.

Bev touched my knee before saying, "Jules, you're not alone anymore. Tell us what she's saying. Between all of us, we have enough resources to help you. It's good that you are taking steps and reporting to your head, but if there is anything we can do to help, we will."

Nodding, I took a deep breath and pulled my phone from my pocket, finding one of the more recent recordings before saying, "I think it's best you just listen, and if I'm making a mountain out of a molehill, tell me."

They crowded closer to me, and I pressed play, hearing Elizabeth's nasally voice over the speaker.

'You're nothing but a fat cow who thinks she's hot stuff now the Crow MC has you

babysitting their whelps. And Rogue, do you honestly think a blimp like you will keep a man like him happy? He's going to get tired of you before long. You're a passing phase with your fat rolls and jiggling arse. Once he's done with you, I'll make sure he sees me. He liked me well enough in secondary school when we fucked. I'm sure I can make him happy again.'

It had been that last bit that had hurt the most until I realised we were in our thirties. Secondary school was far behind us, but she was still living in a fantasy world.

"What the fuck?" Rogue growled, looking at me before his eyes drifted to the phone in my hand.

You could hear a pin drop in the silence. I hadn't realised everyone had been listening to the recording.

"Babe, who the fuck is this woman? I don't know Elizabeth Gaines?" Rogue demanded, looking pissed.

He was definitely Rogue now, not my Marcus.

I shrugged with confusion, "I only know her by that name. I didn't go to school with you guys, so I don't know if she went by another name before."

"What does she look like?" Rea asks me. "If she was in our class, one of us would probably know her. We only had three Elizabeths in our year, so we can narrow it down."

"She's my height with blue eyes and blonde hair. She's very thin and has a small mole on her right cheekbone under her eye."

There was silence, and I could see the guys were thinking hard. We all saw it when it dawned on Draco's face who she was.

"Oh, fuck. It's Bets. And yeah, Rogue never slept with her."

There was a collective round of "Ahs" from Reaper, Dragon, Rogue, and Onyx as the penny dropped.

"Ah, Jesus fuck. You guys and the drama of a small village. Makes me glad I grew up far away from here. I can feel this is going to be a cluster funk… fudge, I mean… fuck," Navy grumbled drunkenly from where he was sitting next to Hawk, who shook his head and handed him a bottle of water.

"Water, brother. You're cut off if you can't say your favourite word," Hawk told him.

"You mean pussy, pussy is my favourite word. I need to get me some. All the women here are hot, but taken. Huh, I may be up for drama if it gets quality pussy," he continued to ramble on but started drinking the water.

We're all laughing at him now. It had broken the tension and taken the focus off me.

Rea let out a drunken giggle and pointed at Draco with a grin, saying, "Oh, I remember her now. She was a crazy bitch in secondary school and mean as hell. Isn't she the one who freaked you out because she called out Rogue's name when you did the deed at some party."

Dragon started laughing. "Yeah, that's right, I remember now. I think we were seventeen or thereabouts, and it was a party at the Rugby Club. She'd been trying it on with Rogue all evening. He told her several times he wasn't interested. So she moved onto you."

"The only reason Rogue wasn't interested was that he only had eyes for Ms Rogers, our science teacher, and she was there that night," Reaper added.

"Ah yes, Ms Rogers," Rogue said a little dreamily as he thought back.

"Oh yeah, Ms Rogers. I have very fond memories of her," Dragon agreed with Rogue and raised his fist for a fist bump which Rogue obliged him with as they grinned at each other.

I laugh at the two of them. "I'm guessing Ms Rogers was every schoolboy's fantasy," I remarked with a smile.

They both nodded and smirked at me.

Dragon answered with a fond smile. "For the two of us, yes, she was. Man, she had these breasts," he held up his hands, showcasing how large her breasts had been. "A well-endowed lady, and her hips." He widens his hands slightly. "Yeah, she was gorgeous with long brown hair and the bluest eyes. She used to wear these pencil skirts with those two-toned heels and ruffled blouses. Or sometimes she'd wear those 1950s dresses with these glasses. Naughty librarian style. Oh yeah, good times. She taught me so much about science," he ended with a snigger.

"Especially biology, I'm guessing," I said dryly, shaking my head.

"Oh, definitely biology," Rea agreed. "I caught Dragon and her going at it backstage at that theatre class we helped with the year after we left secondary school."

Dragon grinned cockily, "Like I said, good times."

"Busy lady," Reaper snorted out a laugh. "Because I'm sure I saw her with you, Rogue, up against her car in the back car park."

"I'm not denying anything," Rogue grinned. "The woman taught Dragon and me a lot that summer, we weren't her students anymore, and she was a little lonely after her divorce. Plus, she was a nice woman. I was nearly eighteen. I wouldn't say no to free pussy, especially, experienced free pussy. Not when she was my every fantasy wrapped up in a nice package. We all knew it wasn't going to be long term. We entered the military, she moved on, and now it's a great memory."

There was a bit more reminiscing from the guys about Ms Rogers, with lots of laughter and teasing thrown in at Dragon and Rogue.

I was glad he hadn't slept with Elizabeth but was a little concerned that she carried the fantasy with her all this time.

"So, help me understand. Elizabeth slept with Draco but pretended it was Rogue?" I queried.

There was a snort from Molly, who muttered into her margarita,
"Figures it would be you to fuck the crazy one," she said, pointing a finger at Draco.

Draco glared at her, "Hey, I didn't know she was crazy at the time. I was seventeen, and all the talk in the changing rooms was that she was fucking amazing in bed. But yeah, it freaked me out when she called out my brother's name as she came. I didn't even get to finish," he grumbled sulkily.

This started another round of teasing. When the hilarity had quieted down. It was Skinny who spoke up from the barbecue area where he'd been cleaning up.

"Reaper, not to butt in, but if she's still obsessed with Rogue nearly fifteen years later, then I think we need to do more checking on her. Can you guys tell me what you know about her, and I'll start researching?"

"Yeah, brother, you're right. We do need to be concerned because, if I remember correctly, wasn't she the one who poked holes in the condoms she carried? Draco, count yourself lucky you didn't finish. Skinny, try Elizabeth Gaines first, I think, she married the guy she trapped by getting pregnant using the faulty condoms."

"Ah fuck, really?" Draco rubbed a shaky hand down his pale face, suddenly all serious. "She tried to get me to use her condoms that night, but you know how Dad was, and he drummed into Onyx and me early on to always use our own."

"Dodged a bullet there, big guy," Molly chirped before taking another sip of her margarita.

Draco glared at her. "You're enjoying this, aren't you?"

"What? Moi?" she asked with a fake gasp, pointing a finger at her chest. "Enjoying the fact that Rogue is being stalked? No, I'm not. But am I enjoying the fact that the high and mighty Draco is actually human and can fuck up like the rest of us? Then yes, I'm enjoying that fact. Although I'm happy that you didn't manage to procreate with her. Because the poor kid, trust me, having a loon-crazy parent is no fun at all. I'd know," she informed him.

Standing up, she put her glass on the table before turning to us with a small bow and a curtesy saying, "Ladies, always a pleasure. We'll do this again next week at my house, sans men. Rogue, talking from experience, you need to report this and keep an eye out. Now that she knows you aren't available, things will escalate. Watch the children. I wouldn't put it past her to use them to get to you."

Then with a flippant *night all,* she walked off towards the road that led to her place next door.

Reaper called out, "Molls, let me get a prospect to drive you home."

From the darkness, she called back, and we saw a flashlight flick on its small beam, lighting up the road. "I'm good, thanks, Reap. I'll call you when I get home. It should only take me ten minutes."

Draco grumbled, getting up. "Stubborn pig-headed woman. Why doesn't she ever listen? Always has to take the hard way."

He stalked off to the quad bikes parked under the trees, climbed on, and drove off towards the light. We listened to their conversation, which was clear in the quiet night. Most of us were trying to hold our laughter in at the two of them, who couldn't seem to agree on anything.

"Molly, get on, and I'll take you home."

"No, thank you, I'm good to walk."

"Jesus, woman, why are you so fucking stubborn. Quit busting my balls and get on the bike."

"Nope, the walk will sober me up."

"Molly, get on the fucking bike. I swear to god, woman, you drive me to drink."

"And I said no thanks, Draco. I'll walk. Plus, you've been drinking."

I could have told him bossing Molly wouldn't get him anywhere, and he must have realised it because, in a softer, gentler tone, he said, "I've had two beers all afternoon,

Molls. Please get on the bike and let me take you home, so I know you are safe."

Her reply brought a round of chuckles from everyone avidly listening to their conversation.

Molly huffed out a breath before replying with a sigh, "Fine. Why didn't you just ask like that in the first place? I think you like irritating me."

She must have gotten on the bike because the next thing we heard was the engine revving and the light disappearing down the road to her house on the property next door.

Reaper stood, pulling Abby up next to him, and tucked her under his arm, "Right, Rogue, I do not like the sound of any of this. Tomorrow, give our PD contact Gary a call. You and Jules can meet him at the police station and make a report. We'll go with Jules to the meeting and take our lawyer with us on Monday. Skinny, find out what you can about this woman and what she's been up to for the last fifteen years. Church tomorrow night at 2100 hours. Don't be late."

With that, he bent his knees, put his shoulder under Abby, and lifted her, making her squeal and laugh.

"Night all," he called out before walking up the path towards the house. Abby berated him all the entire way until we heard what could only be a hand on denim and the faint moans that followed it.

Their leaving broke up the party, and I allowed myself to be pulled up by Rogue and get tucked against his side as we followed Reaper to the house with Onyx and Rea not far behind us.

I was worried about what would happen with Elizabeth on Monday but couldn't help but feel relieved that the MC was behind me.

"It will be okay, babe," Marcus whispered against my head before pressing a kiss there.

I tilted my head against his shoulder to see his face before smiling. Lifting my hand, I caressed his cheek, "How can it not when I have all of you with me?" I answered.

"Exactly," Onyx agreed from behind us. "Not alone anymore, Jules. Although you may want to let your brother know what is going on and have him send Deb and the kids away for a bit."

I stopped walking and turned to Onyx, "Do you think she may go for them?"

Onyx shrugged, "I don't know, but better safe than sorry."

"What about all of you, though? Maybe I should leave. Oh, shit, the kids. Nothing can happen to them. Molly said we needed to watch them."

I was starting to panic, my breaths coming in short gasps as I realised how bad this could be. There were black spots forming, and everything was turning black as I tried to suck in air.

In the back of my mind, I heard Rogue say something, and Rea answered, "She's having a panic attack."

Then Marcus was there, his hand on my face tilting it up to him. Taking my hand, he put it to his chest and whispered soothing words in my ear. As I started to calm down, I could hear what he was saying now that the white noise had disappeared.

"Breath with me beautiful, in and out, that's it. Slower now. Feel my heart. Can you feel it beat for you? In and out."

I matched my breaths to him until I felt my heartbeat slow down and became aware of everyone standing around us.

I was so embarrassed I burst into tears and rested my head against Marcus' chest.

"I should leave," I whispered.

"You're not fucking leaving me, Julia. I've just found you. The kids will be okay. We'll home-school if we have to. It's only three weeks until they break up for the summer. Until then, we'll double up brothers and prospects on all of you. You are not leaving me."

He held me so tight I was struggling to draw a breath again. I had a feeling this had to do with his mother leaving.

Not sure when Noni appeared, the first I realised there were more people around was when Noni touched his shoulder, saying softly, "Marcus, you need to let her breathe. Don't worry, she's not going anywhere, I promise. None of us are," she squeezed her way under his arm, loosening his grip on me and wrapping an arm around his waist and the other around me. Avy burrowed in from the other side, and then Rea pushed in.

"You're not leaving me," he whispered again against my hair.

"I'm not leaving you, honey," I agreed softly.

He relaxed slightly, then chuckled when he realised how many women were hugging him.

"None of us are leaving you, Marcus. Ever," Noni stated, looking her brother in the eye. Her words confirmed what she was thinking.

He nodded, taking a deep breath, "Love you, Noni."

"Love you too, big brother."

"We love you too, Rogue," Avy and Rea said in unison.

He laughed, relaxing his hold on all of us, before saying in amusement, "Brothers, come take your women. I'm taking mine to bed."

Onyx pulled Rea into his arms and started back towards the house. Avy, Hawk, Bull, and Noni disappeared back to the fire after giving us each a hug, and then it was just the two of us standing quietly, arms still wrapped around each other.

"I love you, Jules. Please, all I ask is that if you ever do want to leave, tell me, don't leave me to wonder. But I hope I make you so happy you'll never even think about it."

"I promise I won't ever leave you like that, Marcus. I'm not sure how it happened, but you own my heart, and that is not something I ever thought would happen. I know we've had a lot of seriousness tonight, but I need to tell you something, and if it's a deal breaker, then I'll understand."

"Nothing you tell me will ever stop me from loving you," he declared.

Taking a deep breath, I blurted out, "I can't have children, it was my choice, but I had a hysterectomy two years ago."

I peeked up at him as I told him this, and all I saw was surprise on his face.

"You must have a good reason. I see how you are with the kids at school and ours here, so I know you love kids. But it's not a deal breaker for me. We can be the favourite aunt and uncle. There are tons of kids here, babe, and I'm sure between Reaper and Onyx, there will be more."

"I do love kids, and there was a good reason. But I think that's a conversation for another time. Now I'm bushed, and we have tons to do tomorrow. Let's head to bed."

"Yeah, it's been a day, hasn't it," he agreed.

Turning, we walked back to the house and up to bed. I didn't think I'd be able to get to sleep, but as soon as my head hit my pillow, I was out.

CHAPTER 9

ROGUE

Instead of spending Sunday in bed with my woman, we were traipsing all over the village, filling in paperwork detailing the abuse my woman had been dealing with the last couple of months, and there was a lot. Julia had brought her diary along with the recordings to the police station, and Gary, a friend of the MC, was taking down the report, agreeing to meet us at the school on Monday.

I didn't know how she was still standing, having to listen to that shit day after day, especially while grieving for her dad. It was vile, and I wanted to punch things by the time we left. Julia was her usual kind self, insisting that Elizabeth got help. I'm not sure I would have been so charitable.

After we'd done all that, we headed back to the manor. It was a beautiful afternoon, and the sun was out and shining. So, I'd persuaded Julia to go for a ride.

I knew it would happen. Once a few others realised what we were planning, they decided they wanted to come along. I rolled my eyes. I'd been wanting time alone with Julia but seeing the happiness on her face when Rea and Abby grabbed their helmets after checking if the kids were okay, I knew I wasn't going to get her to myself.

I didn't realise I was grumbling until I felt a pinch through my shirt just above my jeans.

"Ow, woman. What was that for?"

Julia rubbed the smarting spot and said softly, "Stop sulking. I love your family. And I'm glad they're coming with me for my first long ride. It makes me less nervous. You have me to yourself for the rest of our lives."

Wrapping my arm around her waist, I rested my head against the silky softness of her hair and apologised. "You're right, beautiful.

There's no need to be nervous, though, we've gone over everything, and you've been on short rides. I won't let anything happen to you."

Julia smiled up at me before rising on her toes and pressing a kiss to my lips, whispering, "I know you won't."

I heard a wolf whistle as I deepened our kiss. Letting her go, I grinned at Navy, where he sat on his bike waiting with a grin. How the man wasn't hungover, I didn't know.

"Are we doing this or not?" he questioned loudly.

I looked around and saw everyone was mostly ready. Handing Julia her helmet, I remembered how touched she'd been when I'd given it to her a couple of weeks ago when I'd first persuaded her to go out on the bike with me. Each woman had a helmet in their favourite colour with their name scrolled down the side and the MC logo printed on the back. Julia's was a dark burgundy one. If she'd grown up around an MC, she would have realised then how serious I was about her weeks ago. Giving a woman anything with the MC logo was like being given an engagement ring in the normal world. She'd learn, though.

I put on her helmet, then fastened it to make sure it was secure. Julia smiled as she patiently waited for me to do my checks to ensure she was protected. Then, getting on the bike, we waited on Reaper, who was talking to the prospects in the security hut.

Walking back, he stopped at his bike but called out, "We're going to head to Liam's and check on the last club. The one with issues. He wants our opinion on a full refurb and to discuss cameras and security."

We'd agreed just over a month ago to go into business with Noni's ex-in-laws, the O'Sheas, and helped them buy three nightclubs in the two towns bordering our village.

So far, it had been a good investment, and while we were silent partners, they still kept us up to date on what was happening.

Two were doing well, but one wasn't, the books had been checked thoroughly and seemed fine, but the women in the MC still thought something wasn't right. And as they were the ones who dealt with our financials that were all doing very well, we tended to listen when they spoke.

I guessed today was as good a time as any to have a look around as it would be closed, and it was a nice ride through the forest, especially if we went the long way around.

I shouted out to Reaper before he put his helmet on, "Hey, Pres, can we go the long way around?" He nodded and gave a thumbs up over the roar of the bikes starting. Shutting my visor, I waited for Reaper to lead us out, and we all fell into our assigned spots.

It was a good ride, the sun was shining, and the traffic was light, so we kept up a good speed. There was nothing like riding with my brothers. Did we garner looks? Absolutely, but we were used to it and enjoyed our ride as we wended our way down the country roads towards the next town. Julia relaxed about ten minutes in. I could tell by the way she softened against me, and her hands lost their tight grip around my waist.

We'd slowed to a stop at a traffic light, and I looked over at Onyx to see Rea had her phone out and was taking pictures of us.

Out of all the women other than our sisters, she was the most comfortable on the back of a bike, having been riding with Onyx on our property since before he got his licence.

She had her visor up and grinned when she saw me watching before snapping another pick.

Onyx just smiled, his hand resting on her thigh.

They both looked relaxed and happy. I was pleased for them. They'd been through hell and back but now seemed stronger than ever.

That was what I was aiming for with Julia. I wanted that same feeling of contentedness that Onyx and Reaper walked around with.

I knew we'd get there, eventually.

As we pulled away from the lights, I looked at Julia in the wing mirror, her visor was up, and she was smiling hard as she looked around the town we were slowly riding through.

I could see a lot of rides in our future if this was how much she enjoyed what to me was a short one.

Reaper pulled into the back parking at the nightclub, Ozone. Liam was standing at the back doors with them open, waiting for us.

He was grinning wide when he saw us all pull in.

"Now that's a sight," he called out as we parked. "I heard you all coming a mile away."

"Reap," he gave a chin lift as Reaper pulled off his helmet.

"Liam," Reaper nodded back.

I held my hand out for Julia to climb off before I walked my bike back in line with the rest.

Dismounting, I took my helmet off and watched my woman, who looked hot in her tight jeans that cupped her rounded arse, new biking boots, and burgundy leather jacket with the high-vis patches on to match her helmet that I'd bought her. She was undoing her jacket as she walked with Noni and Avy towards the door where Liam was waiting for everyone. Johnny, one of his brothers, came up behind him and clapped him on the shoulder. As soon as he clocked

Julia, I knew because his eyes flared, and he licked his lips.

Yeah, I didn't think so.

I sped up until I was behind the women. I snaked my arm around Julia's waist and pulled her up against me raising my eyebrow at Johnny.

I heard my brothers chuckling behind me. I couldn't help it, I was a possessive fucker who didn't share well, and my girl was gorgeous but completely oblivious.

Johnny grinned good-naturedly, as I knew he would but still managed to piss me off when he took Julia's hand and laid a kiss on it.

"Hello gorgeous, I don't think we've met."

She giggled. Fucking giggled. What was it about the Irish and their charm?

"That's because we haven't." She smoothly removed her hand from his and curled her fingers around the hand I still had on her waist. "I'm Julia, and I'm his."
She tilted her head at me with a wicked smile, squeezed my hand, and walked off toward the girls.

Johnny grinned cockily at me as we both turned and watched her saunter away, her hips rolling with each step.

He sighed wistfully, "You lucky fucker. It's supposed to be the Irish that are lucky, but you Crows seem to keep finding amazing women."

I laughed and shoulder-bumped him, "Good to see you, Johnny. Where have you been?"

"Sorting family, brother. But I'm back now to help Liam with the clubs. Adam is exclusively the security side of the O'Sheas now. I'm sorry I missed all the excitement. Glad it's fucking over now, though. I hate drugs."

"Me too, Johnny, me too." I gestured to our newest members and the prospects who were bringing up the rear.

"Have you met our new brothers and prospects?"

"Can't say I have," he extended his hand to Navy. "Johnny O'Shea."

"This is Navy, Hawk, and the behemoth is Bull. The prospects are Cairo and Blaze."

Once they'd been introduced, we went into the club. It was the first time I'd seen it, and my first impression was it could do with a clean.

The girls agreed with me by the looks on their faces.

Noni's nose was wrinkled as she looked around, "The books showed you pay for a cleaner. I can't see that they do much cleaning."

Just then, Abby came from the back, looking green. Avy was following her, not looking much better.

"Don't go into the bathrooms. They are filthy," Abby said, retching a little but couldn't seem to stop and was fast pushing past us until she hit the doors to outside. Reaper and Rea followed when they heard her being sick.

"Jesus, how bad are they?" Liam queried in alarm.

"They aren't good," Avy said, then smiled. "But I don't think that it's just the bathrooms causing that."

It took us a minute to get what she meant, but Julia suddenly squealed and clapped her hands happily. "She's knocked up."

Avy grinned, just as excited, "Yeah, I think she is. She didn't have any cocktails yesterday because she said she wasn't feeling great. Now I know why. Surprised Reaper let her ride today, though."

"That's because Reaper didn't know he'd knocked up his woman until five minutes ago," Reaper huffed out, coming back inside with his arm around Abby but still managed to glare at her for putting herself and their baby in danger by riding.

"Hey, don't look at me like that. I've only just put two and two together, and we don't know for certain until I take a test. I don't have one, so you'll have to wait until tomorrow," Abby grumbled as she took the water bottle Rea held out to her.

"I've got one in my medical bag back at the Manor, Abbs. We can check when we get home. Although I don't think there's any need, really, we all know you're knocked up," Rea added with a grin.

"Oh, I know for certain," Reaper growled before he puffed his chest out and grinned happily. "I'm going to be a dad."

"You're already a dad, you idiot," Avy said, laughing.

"Yeah, I know, but this time I get to be there from the beginning and all the in-betweens. Five kids," he looked around before saying proudly, "You fuckers are falling behind."

We laughed at him even as Abby grumbled at him. He was an idiot, but we were all happy for them.

Once we'd had a quick look around and seen the state of the place, it made better sense why this one wasn't doing as well as the other two. It needed to be closed, deep cleaned, and refurbished.

Plans were made for Liam and Johnny to come back to the manor with us to discuss a plan. Reaper insisted Abby go back with them in their vehicle.

She'd grumbled but had done it anyway, knowing he was right and that if she was pregnant, a car was safer than on the back of his bike, no matter how carefully he rode.

CHAPTER 10

JULIA

Yawning, I snuggled down into our pillows on the bed, waiting for Marcus to finish showering and come to bed. It had been a busy day, between logging reports with the police, our bike ride, and discussing the refurb of the nightclub. I groaned a little, thinking of tomorrow. I was not looking forward to it.

I was just drifting off when he switched off the bathroom light and walked naked into our bedroom. I watched him through slitted lids, the light playing across the muscles that flexed as he reached up to hang the towel on the rail to dry. I couldn't believe that he was mine. Mine to touch and to love. The man was hot from his red hair that he kept a little long and always had a ruffled look because he had a habit of running his hands through it right down to his feet.

Like all the men of the MC, he was tall and muscular. They all kept up a training regime, and sometimes if I got up early enough, I could watch them run drills around the property then they spent hours at the gym the MC owned.

I rolled over on my back, the sheets tucked securely under my arms as my eyes travelled up his legs as he walked over to the bed. They came to a stop at his cock, which was hard, long, and thick, standing up against his muscled stomach. Licking my lips, I moaned at the sight and squirmed restlessly on the bed.

Marcus gripped his cock hard, so hard the head turned purple as pre-ejaculate wet the top before stopping at the edge of the bed. Looking at me through hooded eyes, his eyes travelled down my form encased in the sheet. "See something you like, beautiful?" he growled throatily.

"Yes," I whispered.

"Do you want this?" he asked, slowly moving his hand up and down his cock.

I nodded.

"Need words, baby."

I took a deep breath before answering, gathering my courage, "Yes, Marcus, I want your cock."

He grinned at me, "See, that wasn't so hard, was it?"

I shook my head while watching him.

"If you want my cock, baby, you have to let go of the sheet."

My fingers flexed as I slowly let go of my death grip on the sheet.

Marcus knelt on the bed and slowly pulled the sheet down until my breasts were bare to the night. I breathed in a shaky breath. This was still hard for me to be naked in front of him. No matter how many times he told me I was beautiful, my head still messed with me.

"You're thinking too much, Julia," his words brought my attention back to him to find him looking at me, his face soft. Then with a wicked grin, he told me, "I guess I'm going to have to keep you so busy coming that you'll forget about everything else but me."

With that, he pulled the sheet completely off my body, making me squeak in surprise. I automatically used my hands to try to cover myself.

"Uh uh, don't try to hide my treasures from me. Otherwise, I'm going to take these," he took my hands and pulled them above my head, "and tie them to those," he nodded to the headboard.

I tilted my head back and saw the metal circles embedded in the headboard. I'd thought they were a decorative part of the bed. Marcus pulled at one, and it pulled out of the headboard. I swallowed and turned my attention back to him.

"I don't think I'm ready for that," I whispered.

"Then don't hide from me. There is nothing about you I don't love."

Taking my one hand, he lifted it to the ring, wrapping my fingers around it, and then did the same with the other hand.

"Hold tight and don't let go until I tell you. If you do, you don't get to come. Understand, beautiful?"

I nodded my head, my eyes on his face.

"Words, beautiful," he reminded me.

"Yes, Marcus, I won't let go," I promised him.

"Good girl," he praised before lowering his mouth to my ear, nipping it with his teeth, making me shudder at the nip of pain before he whispered, "Scream as hard as you want, beautiful. Nobody can hear you. We're alone up here."

I gasped at his words before swallowing, both nervous and turned on by him.

His mouth travelled down my body, paying special attention to both my breasts until my nipples were so hard they were painful. I shuddered when he got to my pussy. I knew I was wet, wetter than I'd ever been. I could feel it coating my thighs.

Marcus pushed open my thighs, and I watched as he licked his lips before his eyes lifted to mine, and he grinned wickedly at me.

"Look at this beautiful pussy, baby," he swiped his fingers through my folds and held up a wet glistening finger. "All this for me. Let's see if I can make more." He sucked his finger into his mouth. Getting off the bed, he pulled something out from under the bed and then looked up, "Don't let go of those rings, beautiful. They'll stretch."

Wrapping his arms around my thighs, he pulled me to the bottom of the bed and put my feet on what could only have been a ledge. Then, pushing my thighs apart, he knelt and breathed in.

"Mmm, you smell delicious," he growled before running his tongue up the inside of my thighs. My hips rose, and he gripped them tight, holding me down as he ran his tongue around my hard clit. I whimpered as I felt my orgasm building and moaned in disappointment when he lifted his head.

"No coming until I say you can," he ordered.

I moaned as he again ran his tongue through my folds and then pushed it deep inside me.

I wasn't sure how he didn't want me to come. This felt too good to not come.

He continued to suck and lick me until I was a shaking mess on the bed, trying my best to hold off my orgasm, but I couldn't. My breaths came in gasps. I felt like I was going to explode. I pleaded, "Marcus, I can't hold it. Please, I need to come."

"You only had to ask, sweetheart."

Gently he thrust one finger, then two, into me as he sucked hard on my clit. I came hard. I could feel wetness gushing from me as he lapped at me until I couldn't take anymore and my thighs closed around his head. My body shuddered. I felt tears on my cheeks and wanted to wipe them but daren't, remembering his words about not letting go of the rings.

Feeling a muscled chest rest against my upraised knees, I looked down my body at Marcus leaning against me, his big hands rubbing up and down my sides.

"You come so beautifully, baby. Well done for not letting go of the rings. I think you deserve a reward."

"Your cock?" I whispered hopefully.

He grinned at me, "Not yet, baby, but soon though."

I moaned, rubbing my thighs together. I needed to be filled.
He pressed a kiss to my knee. "Shh, I'll take care of that ache in a minute. Now don't let go of the rings."

With no warning, I gasped in surprise as he flipped me over on the bed until I was kneeling on the ledge that my feet had been on with my upper body resting on the bed.

I didn't have time to think about how this new position had me exposed to his gaze.

I looked over my shoulder at him, his hands resting on my hips as he took in my new position. Rubbing his hands up and down my sides, he then caressed his fingers over my hips.

He whispered to me, "Do you know how long I've fantasised about having you like this in my bed?" Marcus gently pushed a finger into me, and I couldn't help but thrust back against it.

"Oh yeah, sweetheart, just like that. I want you to fuck yourself on my fingers until you come."

"I don't know if I can come again," I hissed as he added another finger to my already sensitised pussy.

"You can," he assured me.

I heard a buzz, and his other hand disappeared under me to my clit. I had no clue where he'd got the vibrator from, but as soon as he pressed it to my clit I was thrusting back against his fingers, my orgasm coming out of nowhere. I felt a trickle down the inside of my thighs as I gushed, groaning and sobbing. I pressed my face into the bed as I came and came. It felt like the waves would never stop.

Just as I was coming down, Marcus thrust his cock hard into me, his hands gripping my hips with bruising force as his thrusts sped up faster and harder. He pounded into me harder than I'd ever been taken before. I lifted myself on my elbows and thrust back against him. I loved how hard he was hammering into me. I clenched around him just as another orgasm hit and felt the wet spurts of his cum coat my walls.

My arms collapsed under me, our breaths rasping out, Marcus' heaviness where he leaned against my back.

I sighed shakily as he softened and slowly slipped from my body. He lifted off me, and I felt something soft between my thighs, wiping our combined cum from our bodies.

"I need to investigate this bed and see what else it's hiding," I said drowsily, sleep fast approaching.

I heard him chuckle then his fingers enclosed mine that was still clutching the rings.

"You can let go now, beautiful."

Letting go of the rings, I watched as he let them slip back into the headboard. Huh? They'd been on springs.

I crawled back up the bed and collapsed on our pillows in a boneless mess, completely naked and not caring at all. He'd shown me in countless ways he loved me just as I was. I needed to start believing it for myself.

The bed moved a little as Marcus got in. Pulling the sheet up over us, he softly kissed my shoulder before pulling me tight against him as sleep took me.

CHAPTER 11

ROGUE

I woke up hard and horny, feeling like I was about to come. Opening my eyes, I looked down my body to find Julia kneeling on the bed between my legs, her mouth hot and wet around my cock, her long hair drawn over one shoulder brushing the tops of my thighs, her brown eyes heavy-lidded as she watched me before lowering them as she moved her mouth down my shaft.

I let out a deep groan as I thrust up into her mouth. She took all of me.

"Oh, fuck baby. Your mouth feels so good."

Reaching down, I threaded my fingers through her hair, holding her head still as I thrust up. Trying to slow my thrusts when all I wanted to do was rush to the finish.

Her hands were on my thighs, holding me down, and that's when I realised my woman was taking my entire length and not gagging.

"Fuck me, I'm a lucky fucker," I whispered hoarsely as she swallowed. Her throat closed around my cock. I groaned as I gently pulled her head up and off my shaft.

"What's wrong?" she asked huskily, her lips puffy and red from where they'd been wrapped around my cock.

"Nothing, baby, but I'm about to come, and want to come inside you."

"I was enjoying myself," she muttered a little sulkily.

I grinned, pulling her up next to me and tapping her thigh, saying, "Up."

Julia shook her head, "No, Marcus, I'm too heavy!"

I tapped the flat of my hand firmly against her thigh. She looked at me with wide, shocked eyes.

"Beautiful, I've told you. To me, you're perfect. I'm a big guy. There is no way you are too heavy for me. Now up, I want to feel you on my cock."

Still looking uncertain, I settled her over my hips, her wet folds resting on my hardness. I thrust up against her, hitting her clit, and that look of uncertainty faded away as she lifted up and lowered back down on my cock. Her walls encased me as she clenched before releasing me and rising up again before lowering back down. She did this several times, clenching and releasing me with the walls of her pussy until I was about ready to burst. I wasn't sure what the fuck she was doing, but it felt amazing.

I watched her face as she concentrated on me, her lips lifting in a smug smile as she watched my face. I knew I was not far from coming, and there was no way I was coming without her. I knew she was close. I could feel her dripping down my balls. That was how wet she was.

Licking my thumb, I found her clit and circled it. Her hips stuttered slightly before they continued, only a little faster this time. I added a little more pressure, and she came. I let go pounding up into her holding her thighs tight. So tight I was sure she would have bruises. She took everything I was giving her.

When I stopped coming, I opened my eyes to see a smug Julia leaning back against the knees I'd raised to get more traction.

I grinned happily at her. "Baby, feel free to wake me like that every morning."

Smiling, she leaned forward, her heavy breasts rubbing against my chest, her long hair surrounding us. I wrapped my hands in the long length pulling her down and taking her mouth in a wet kiss.

"Love you, Julia."

She smiled softly, rubbing her fingers across my brows and then down my cheeks, before running her nose up my cheek towards my ear, "Love you too, Marcus."

I would have stayed like that all day, but I knew we couldn't. It was my turn to drive the boys to the gym. We'd settled into taking it in turn if Aunt Maggie couldn't do it. Just then, there was a knock on the door, and Ben called out softly.

"Rogue, are you still okay with taking us to the gym?"

Clearing my throat, I answered, "Yeah, Ben. Give me ten, and I'll be out."

"Okay."

We heard his footsteps fall away.

"Oh, God, Rogue, do you think he heard us?"

I shrugged, "I don't know, baby. But I wouldn't worry about it."

"Ugh, that's such a bloke thing to say," she grumbled as she lifted herself from me and collapsed on the bed.

Getting out of bed, I pulled her up from the bed and took her into the shower with me. I couldn't take my time like I wanted to as I knew the boys were waiting, so I rushed through my shower finishing before Julia. Still, I took the vision of her with her head thrown back, her long brown hair wet, and her arms raised as she pushed the water back off her face, lifting her heavy breasts high, water dripping off the tips of her nipples. I left our room with my cock hard again like I hadn't just come.

My brothers were smirking at me as I walked out the kitchen door and swung my gym bag towards Ben, who grabbed it and put it in the car.

"Running late today, brother?" Draco taunted me.

"Yep," I agreed, not taking the bait before continuing. "And I'm feeling nice and relaxed. That's more than any of you fuckers, except maybe Reaper and Onyx, can say. And Bull, if you and my sister got it on, I don't want to know, or you Hawk with Avy."

Opening the door of the Range Rover, I handed my cut off to Alec, who was in the front to hold it for me, before turning to Draco. "And Draco, if you'd stop pissing your woman off long enough, you might be feeling as good as me."

Giving him a wide grin as I got into the vehicle.

"Fuck you, Rogue," he held up both hands with middle fingers raised.

I laughed as I pulled away. The three teenage boys were smiling at our exchange.

It was good for them to see how we interacted and to learn from it. I would do anything for my brothers, as would they for me.

CHAPTER 12

JULIA

I was feeling pretty good about myself with new confidence when I met Rogue in the reception at school before my meeting with the headteacher of our school.

I stifled a laugh at our receptionist Laurie who was waving her hand next to her face and mouthing *'Hot'* to me when Marcus bent to kiss my cheek. This was followed by her giving two thumbs up. Only for it to be ruined by Elizabeth barging into the reception and literally pushing me out of the way.

"Rogue," she whispered in a sultry voice, putting her slim hand with bright red nails on his chest. "I haven't seen you in a while. How have you been?" she purred, moving closer.

I raised my eyebrows at her blatant come-on. Rogue, to his credit, pulled her hand from him and moved behind me, slipping his arm around my waist.

"Bets," he nodded.

She scowled, her face turning red before snapping at him, "It's Elizabeth, not Bets. I haven't been Bets in a long time."

"Doesn't seem like you've changed much from the Bets we all knew," he returned in a dry tone.

I kept quiet, knowing if I said anything, it would only set her off, and I didn't want that in the school reception.

She shrugged, reached out, and ran her hand down his free arm.

"Anyway, do you fancy meeting up for a drink later? We used to have such a good time in our final year at secondary school."

I gaped at her audacity. There I was, standing within the circle of Marcus' arm, and she was hitting on him. Laurie was watching the goings on in glee, and I just knew what would be the talk of the teachers' lounge at break time.

Rogue again moved his arm away from her touch before saying with a sneer, "One, we were never a thing in school. You didn't even register on my radar. Two, I'd never go where one of my brothers has been, and three, why would I even look at you when I have perfection in my bed every night?"

Up until then, I don't even think she'd registered me. She'd been completely focused on Rogue and whatever fantasy she had built up in her mind about them.

It was a little scary to be faced with her complete obsession with him. I shifted uncomfortably in Marcus' arms when I became part of her focus. Her eyes narrowed to slits as she angrily noticed his arm around me.

Her face turned red as she spat at me, "You! I warned you to stay away from him. He's mine! He's always been mine!"

She was raging, her face getting redder, spittle running down her chin. Her long fingernail jabbed me painfully in the chest.

Rogue moved me behind him, taking the brunt of her anger. Just then, the bell rang for the end of class, and I knew before long, the corridors would be filled with the kids changing classes. I didn't want them to see this. Laurie must have had the same thought because she'd headed off towards the offices when Elizabeth had started, and she and the head teacher were hot-footing it back to the reception area.

"Ms Gaines," Carl Simpson, the head teacher, bellowed to get her attention.

It stopped the vitriol she was spewing, and she turned to him, fury on her face and his interruption.

Thankfully just then, the MC lawyer and Gary, the police contact and friend of the Crow MC, buzzed at the security door. Laurie quickly let them in. Gary took one look at the scene and immediately restrained Elizabeth. Laurie and I rushed to pull the blinds down on the corridor windows just as the kids started spilling into the hall.

We watched in silence. Tension was high as he called it in on the radio. Ten minutes later, statements were taken, and Elizabeth was removed from the school. We moved to the head teacher's office for the meeting, which was over and done with quickly, considering what he'd witnessed. All the evidence I'd gathered, including the report I'd made to the police, was taken.

"I'm so sorry this happened, Julia. I wish you'd come forward sooner. I need to check with my other staff to see if she's upset anyone else," Carl said.

Then our usually put-together head paled. He ran his fingers through his hair and groaned, rubbing his hands down his face.

"Shit, that's why Lacey left last year. I need to call her," he muttered, standing and moving to the door to let us all out.

"Thanks for bringing this to my attention. If you are, god forbid, ever in this position again, you need to let me know. You're one of our best teachers, and I don't want to lose you," he said sincerely before I left his office.

Smiling, I patted his shoulder, "Don't worry, I'm not going anywhere. I love the kids, and I've always enjoyed working here. It would take more than a man-obsessed, unwell woman to make me leave."

He huffed out a laugh and shook his head before shaking Rogue and then Gary's hand.

I walked them back out to reception, where we found Alec, Ben, and Sam waiting for us.

Checking the clock, I saw it was lunchtime. "What are you three doing here," I asked.

"Waiting for you to make sure you're okay," Alec replied before continuing, "We were on the sports field when we saw Ms Gaines being taken away and knew something had happened. You're ours. We needed to make sure you were okay."

"Plus, Bren demanded it, and she can get pretty scary when she's mad. She'd be here, but she's helping in art with the art club today," Sam explained.

My heart warmed and melted at the concern shown to me by the MC kids. I loved spending time with all of them. They were awesome young people.

Rogue looked proud of them as he offered each of them his fist for a fist bump.

"Proud of you boys," he told them. "It's all good, we'll explain more at home, but I do want you to keep an extra eye on the girls for me for now, and if you see anything suspicious, let one of us know."

"Will do, Rogue," they answered and picked up their bags from where they'd been lying at their feet.

"Ms Julia." I got a nod and a grin from each of them as they left the reception. We watched the three of them leave with the same confident swagger in their step that they'd picked up from the men in the MC. I grinned a little when I noticed some of the girls checking them out as they walked past. Rogue gave a little chuckle seeing the same thing I was.

"Guess I'm going to have to remind Gunny and Reaper to have a talk with them," he muttered quietly.

I sniggered and replied with a grin. "I'm so glad I never have to have that conversation."

Rogue pressed a kiss to my forehead. "I better go and update Reaper. See you in a few hours, gorgeous. Keep safe."

"You too, honey," I replied, turning to watch as he opened the door and swaggered up the path towards the car park. His arse looked awesome in his tight jeans, his cut hitting just above the waist, the Crow MC insignia bright in the June sunshine. Laurie came and stood next to me as he walked away.

"You are one lucky bitch, Jules," she said with a dreamy sigh.

I gave a surprised laugh. "Laurie, I don't think I've ever heard you swear. And thank you, I am a lucky bitch, and I know it."

Turning, I left the reception area with a bounce in my step.

Today could have gone worse. I hoped Elizabeth got the help she needed.

CHAPTER 13

ROGUE

What a fucking day. I couldn't believe Bets. It was like she didn't see Julia when she was coming on to me in the school reception. There was something seriously wrong there. I couldn't help but feel this wasn't the end of it, and we would have issues again before long.

For now, we'd been called to Church, and Skinny had found out more information that needed to be shared.

I was in my place at the table, waiting for the rest of my brothers to get there. The first to trickle in was Draco. I took one look at his scowling face and knew he'd been to the property next door. He was also soaking wet.

"What's she done now, brother?" I asked him.

He stood at his chair, hands on his hips, head down, scowling at the table, dripping water on the floor.

"I swear, Rogue, that woman was put on this earth to test me," he grumbled. "I went over because I'd overheard her tell Avy she had a leak at the barbecue last weekend. When I knocked on the door, I asked if it still needed doing, and she immediately took it as though I thought she wasn't capable and couldn't pick up the phone to call a plumber. The fuck of it was she was soaking wet, and the water was fucking squirting out the pipe like a geyser while she was arguing with me. She looked like a drowned rat." He grinned at the memory.

I bit back a chuckle, thinking he didn't look much better.

"I hope you didn't tell her that."

"Fuck no, I don't have a death wish. I did laugh a little, though."

He grinned wider.

"So, is it fixed?" I asked, knowing there was no way he'd leave her like that.

"Of course it is." Draco glared at me. "I wouldn't leave her like that no matter how much she pisses me off."

Navy, Hawk, Bull, and Dragon had come in while he was telling me and were shaking their heads as they listened to his tale. We could all see where this was going, and when the two of them finally got it together, it would be explosive. Although the two of them fighting seemed almost like foreplay to them.

Reaper came in with Skinny behind him, looked at our grinning faces and a wet Draco, held up his hand, and stated, "I don't want to fucking know."

Bond knocked on the door and stood in the opening, holding a towel. Draco walked over, took it, and started drying himself off.

"Bond, get the rest of the prospects, lock and secure the main gate. I want you all in this meeting. If anyone needs us, they can use the intercom or call us. On your way back, check in the kitchen for the old fucks and tell them Church is starting in ten minutes, and if they're not here, originals or not, they are being fined," Reaper ordered.

He turned to Skinny, who was still standing in the doorway, "Skinny, take the seat next to Bull and set up."

"Yes, Pres," he said with a nod and did as asked.

Navy was adding the additional chairs we needed at the table. It felt good to see the table full.

The rest of the brothers and prospects trickled in, and ten minutes later, we all sat ready to find out what this was all about.

Reaper hit the gavel on the table calling the meeting to order.

"Well, I was hoping we'd have a nice quiet summer now that the ACES are done with. But it doesn't look like it. The prospects are in on this meeting because they need to be aware of what's going on. Skinny, tell us what you found out."

We turned and looked at him, but he was so focused on his screen that he didn't notice until Bull tapped his arm.

Looking up, he cleared his throat before stating, "Sorry, Pres. Elizabeth Gaines also know as Bets Green, born in London to a typical middle-class family, moved here with her family for a fresh start when she was eight.

"This was after her twin sister drowned falling into the Thames on a day out. At the time, there had been some speculation that it wasn't an accident, but there has never been any proof. Her parents didn't believe the few onlookers that said they'd seen her pushed in by her sister Bets. They came here to make a fresh start after Bets was hurt at school, coming home with bruises. The child that was accused denied that they'd hit Bets hard enough to cause the bruises. However, during the school investigation, another child from the class above hers came forward to say they'd seen Bets throwing herself into the door frame and banging her head on it, which is what caused the bruises.

"Her parents found her help, assuming her behaviour was grief from losing her twin. For a few years, she seemed fine until the last year in secondary school." He paused, clicking a few more buttons before turning the laptop around for us to see the pictures. "When her obsession with Rogue started."

"I tracked down a friend of hers from school. Reaper and I went and saw her this morning. She told us that Bets was obsessed and would secretly take pictures of Rogue, cut his head out, and glue them to pictures with her in them. She used to play it off as a joke, but the friend still had one in a box of mementoes she'd kept. I scanned it in before we took it to the police to add to the evidence."

The picture was of a young Bets and me. She'd cut my entire body out of another picture and stuck it next to her. There were hearts drawn all around the picture.

I shuddered, completely creeped out, feeling like I was going to throw up.

"This is the guy she married and had a child with. Do you see the similarities?" Skinny clicked another button, and the screen changed to show us a young, well-built guy with red hair. He could have been a close cousin if we'd been standing next to each other.

"Fuck," I swore. "This is getting way too fucking creepy."

There were noises of agreement from around the room.

"Are they still married?" Dragon asked.

Skinny shook his head. Turning his laptop back to him, he continued. "No, they divorced when the baby was three months old, non-contested. They had a baby girl who was born early when Bets fell down the stairs at home. She was by herself.

"There are notes from concerned health officials in the hospital that she wasn't bonding with the baby, and postnatal depression was noted. Then when the baby had been home six weeks after spending nearly a month in the NICU for being born early, the father came home early to hear the baby screaming from the bathroom. Rushing upstairs, he found the child in the bathtub with the water running, nearly covering the baby's face. Bets was standing in the bathroom watching the water inch up, doing nothing.

"He got the baby out and to the hospital to be checked. Thankfully, she was okay, and he'd arrived in time. It was all documented. Bets went to a mental health facility for the next two years to get treatment. He got a divorce and sole custody of their daughter." Skinny again turned the laptop around to show us a picture of the same guy, older now, with his arm around the shoulders of a beautiful red-headed girl in her early teens. They were both smiling wide and happy at whoever was taking the picture.

"I called him on the number Skinny found, and we had a long chat," Reaper informed us. "He seems like a good guy from our conversation. He remembered all of us. They now live up north. He married again when his girl was two, and they had two other children. He's happy, but he did have a word of warning that we need to be careful as Bets is good at manipulation, and wherever she's gone, it won't be long until she's out. He thinks she's dangerous, she's just never been caught other than the time with their daughter, and that was put down to post-natal depression. We'll keep monitoring her, and I've let our contact in the local PD know what we've found. They've also spoken to her ex-husband.

"From today, I need another brother or prospect to accompany Rogue and Abby when they collect the kids from school. Get your names to Dragon, who can make a schedule at the end of this meeting. I'll go with them this afternoon. Rogue, you and Julia don't go anywhere without having another brother or two with you."

I tilted my chin in agreement.

Reaper continued. "Sorry, brother, I know the two of you like to go for bike rides. You'll have to have an escort until we know what's happening with Bets."

"That's good with me, Pres," I agreed without hesitation. There's no way I'd put Julia at risk.

"Right, until we know more, heads on a swivel and an additional eye out when you're on the women and kids. They'll all be getting escorted from here on out. Luckily our women are sensible and won't kick up a fuss. Except maybe Molly," Reaper grinned at Draco.

"Fuck off, Reap. Don't look at me. Have Hawk or Navy or hell, even one of the prospects tell her. She doesn't seem to mind them," he muttered grumpily.

We laughed at his disgruntlement.

"That's because we don't piss her off when we go over to sort the pigs out," Navy informed him.

"I don't mean to piss her off. No matter what comes out of my mouth, it sets her off. It can be a compliment, and she'll take it as an insult," he objected sourly.

"Well, I guess telling her, her beer was just okay, even if it was homebrew when that's her business, didn't help," Dragon chuckled.

Draco threw up his hands in frustration. "How the fuck was I supposed to know she owned a brewery and the homebrew in her kitchen was a new line she was experimenting with? You all only know because Avy told Hawk, who told Bull, and so on. For some reason, none of you fucks told me."

He glared at us.

I couldn't help but chuckle. None of us had realised he didn't know Molly owned a brewery. He hadn't been around when Avy mentioned it to Hawk for some reason. Draco had opened his big mouth, insulting Molly's beer. We hadn't purposely kept it from him. The whole situation was fucking hilarious, though, and kept us endlessly amused.

"Okay," Reaper called out, bringing us back to order. "Now that we know all the ways Draco is cocking up with his woman, we have other things to discuss. Like additional security for the fair in two weeks. I'm thinking of asking Liam and his guys to help out. Is everyone good with that?"

A round of ayes went around the table in agreement.

"Right, now that's done, prospects can leave. Skinny, thanks for the intel," Reaper informed them as they stood and left.

Once they were out of Church, Reaper said, "We need to vote on the prospects. They have done more than the three months we initially mandated, and I have no issue with any of them. How do the rest of you feel?"

"I'm good with voting, Pres," Gunny called out. "Blaze was very helpful when we dropped that last fucking ACE in London, and he never stares at my woman like she's a piece of steak." This last bit was said with a glare at Navy.

Navy threw up his hands as if in surrender. "Ah, come on, Gunny, you know I don't mean anything by it. And I don't do it anymore now that I've got used to her. Besides, that woman is all about you and her boy. I don't think she notices anyone else." Navy smirked at Gunny, who just shook his head and sighed at our brother.

Once we all stopped laughing at the two of them. The votes were cast for the rest of the prospects. And it was a unanimous yes to all of them becoming full brothers.

"Okay, so when do you all want to do the ceremony?" Reaper asked.

"How about next weekend," Hawk offered. "Avy is having a karaoke night at the pub, we can do the ceremony in the afternoon, and they can let loose that night to celebrate.

We'll all be there so we can keep an eye out."

"I second that," I agreed.

That brought the meeting to an end. On hearing about the karaoke, I started to plan but needed to speak to Avy, Noni, and Rea first to see if they were on board to help me.

I was concerned about what was happening with Bets. But I was also more content now than ever, and the constant itch to be on the move had left me. It was the first time in my life I didn't feel the need to roam.

My woman grounded me like no other.

CHAPTER 14

JULIA

The past week since Elizabeth was removed from the school had been peaceful and fun. I felt a lot more confident in myself, not just as a teacher but as a woman, and it had been noticed by my fellow staff members and my family.

I had supper with Warren and Deb last night. Marcus had said he had some MC stuff to do, so I'd gone alone. Although, I had been escorted there by Hawk as he was on his way to the pub to spend the evening with Avy. I needed to call Reaper when I was ready to leave and get an escort home.

Deb had grinned at me, her eyes sparkling brightly when she'd opened the front door as I'd pulled up in the new car that Marcus had insisted he'd buy me. My old Ford was being used to teach older kids how to drive.

"Well, my lovely sister-in-law, don't you look amazing," Deb gushed.

I grinned back at her and looked down at what I was wearing. It was just a pair of denim shorts, sandals, and a new flowing top, but my arms were left bare. Until recently, I'd have covered them up as I'd thought they were too fat.

"I feel good," I replied, enfolding her in a hug.

Her bump was a lot more pronounced now. I smiled when I felt something push up against me. Looking down, I could see her tight T-shirt move a little.

"Wow, she's a busy little bean, isn't she?" I smiled.

Deb grabbed my hand, pulling it tight against her belly. We grinned at each other as I felt a kick.

"That she is," Deb said, pulling me into the house. "Come on, supper is nearly ready. You need to tell me about this glow you have going on before your brother and the boys come back from football."

"Do you want a glass of wine?" she asked, heading to the fridge.

"Sure," I replied, dumping my bag on a chair in the lounge and joining her in the kitchen. "Is there anything you need help with?"

"Nah," she replied, handing me a glass of white. "Sit, tell me about all this," she said, waving her hands up and down me.

Smiling wide at her and then laughing when she sat down at the breakfast bar in front of me, folding her hands under her chin and looking at me eagerly.

I shrugged a little before replying, "I don't know what glow you mean. I'm just really happy. School is better than ever, and living with Rogue is amazing. He makes me feel good about myself. He's always telling me I'm beautiful, and I'm finally starting to believe it."

"That's because you are," Deb interrupted before allowing me to continue.

"I've started going to the gym after school with the kids, and Carly is working with me on a routine. I'm really enjoying it. The student is now the teacher."

I shake my head a little on the last bit, Deb laughing. She knew how much I hated going to the gym before.

"What's different about going to the gym this time?" she asked curiously.

"I don't know, maybe it's the fact that it's owned by the Crows, and I feel protected there. It also isn't a fancy gym like the one I went to before. There are no mirrors in this one. It really is just for working out or beating the crap out of each other in the ring, like they all seem to like doing. Then there are the MC kids. They make it fun, and nobody stares at me or comments about me being a hippo and that I shouldn't be there."

Deb looked furious at my comment on how I'd been treated at previous gyms.

Patting my hand, she commented, "Oh babe, I hate that you've had to put up with arseholes. And I'm glad you're happy. I wish that you could have seen before how gorgeous you are. And I'm beyond thrilled that you have a man who sees how wonderful you are. You're the best sister-in-law and aunty anyone could wish for."

I blinked furiously to stop the tears welling in my eyes from falling.

"Oh, Deb, I'm so glad my brother married you."

She grinned cheekily at me and waved her hand up and down her body while saying, "Me too. I mean, how was he going to resist all this awesomeness."

I snorted out a laugh and grabbed a tissue from the box on the counter, wiping at my eyes before taking a big swig of my wine. Deb left me to gather myself while she pulled a bubbling lasagne out of the oven and put the garlic bread in.

Turning back from the stove, she asked, "So, where is your man tonight?"

"He had something on with the MC," I answered just as the front door crashed open, and my two nephews came barrelling in with shouts of, "Aunty Julia, you're here."

I smiled, slipping off my stool. I waited with my arms open as my nephews headed to me. I enfolded them in tight hugs, wrinkling my nose a little at the smell of a sweaty little boy. My brother grinned at the look on my face.

"Hey, Jules," he greeted, dropping a kiss on my head as he passed me to get to his wife.

"You've got a new car, Aunty Jules," Julian, my eldest nephew named after me, says.

"Yep," I agreed with a nod. "Your Uncle Dragon decided I needed a new one."

"It's awesome," David, my youngest nephew, agreed before turning to his mum and asking, "Is supper ready yet? I'm starving."

I turned my attention from my nephews to see my brother letting Deb up for air from where he'd had her pressed against the kitchen counter. I grinned a little as Julian rolled his eyes when he noticed them.

"Yes, Davy, it's nearly ready, you boys go wash up, and then we'll eat," Deb instructed them.

They thundered up the stairs pushing and shoving each other to get to the bathroom first. Typical little boys.

I spent the rest of the evening enjoying dinner with my family and catching up with the boys on what was going on in their lives.

It was a good night that ended up better when Rogue arrived unexpectedly just before I was leaving. The kiss he laid on me made the boys groan, "Gross Uncle Rogue, that's my aunty. You're as bad as dad is with mum," Julian grumbled.

Rogue grinned at them. "Boys, one day, when you find a woman as awesome as your aunt or mum, you'll get it."

"Nope," David objected, "I'm never kissing girls. I don't like them, except Ellie she's okay, she never asks stupid questions and doesn't mind playing football with us at break time."

"Is Ellie in your class?" Rogue asked.

David nodded his head excitedly. "Yeah, she moved to our class last week. She sits next to me."

I made a mental note to speak to Abby as David was in accelerated classes for students working above where they were expected to be at their age. It was an experiment the junior school was running. They'd found that children who were finishing work quicker than others were getting bored and misbehaving. At the beginning of the school year, when it was least noticeable, they'd moved all the kids around and started giving them different work. From what I could understand, it was working well. They continued to test during the year and moved the children up if needed. I knew my nephew was much happier at school because of this system.

"What are you doing here?" I asked Marcus as I leaned closer to him, his arms now loose around my waist.

"I needed to see your brother about something, and I missed you," he replied.

My heart melted. That was one thing about the men in the MC. They weren't shy about letting anyone know how they felt about them.

Letting me go, he looked at Warren and asked, "You got time to come outside a bit? I need your opinion on something."

"Sure," Warren agreed, standing up from the dining table. "Boys, clear the table for your mum and aunt."

"Sure, Dad." Julian got up and started piling plates. Davy got up to help, and before long, the two of them were in the kitchen arguing about who was washing up and who was drying.

I smiled. It brought back memories of Warren and me arguing about the same damn thing. Deb shook her head as she listened to them, rolling her eyes. "I'm sure I argued about the same thing with my sister," she muttered.

I laughed, "I was just thinking the same thing," I admitted.

"So what do you think Rogue wants with Warren?" Deb questioned.

I shrugged. "Not sure. They were discussing building a couple of cottages as they may take on more prospects. So it could be about that."

Just then, the door opened, and Marcus and Warren came back in. Talking about the karaoke night at the pub this weekend.

"You and Deb should come out with us," Rogue invited, pulling the chair out next to me and sitting down.

Warren looked at Deb, who nodded easily. "Sure, if we can get a sitter for the evening."

"Okay, if we can get a sitter, we'll be there," Warren confirmed.

The boys finished in the kitchen and found the cake Deb had baked earlier, shouting out if they could have a piece.

"Hey mum, can we have some of this cake," Julian shouted from the kitchen.

"Sure," Deb agreed. "Bring it out here with some plates, and we'll all have some."

The rest of the evening passed with us chatting. The boys kept us entertained with stories from school. Before long, it was bath and bedtime for them, so Marcus and I got up to leave.

After hugging and kissing everyone, I walked out to my car to see that Bond was waiting for us. I got in and waited for Marcus to get on his bike before pulling out behind him and Bond to follow them home.

Ugh, bloody Elizabeth was a pain in the arse.

I kept forgetting we had to have escorts every time we left the manor. Luckily I didn't really go anywhere. I was mostly either at school or home. This could get old fast, though. I wondered how long we'd have to do this?

CHAPTER 15

ROGUE

It had only been a week of having to always have one of my brothers with me when I rode out, and it was starting to wear on me.

I was a loner by nature, and having the restrictions while I understood them was chafing at my temper. We'd not seen hide nor hair of Bets. She had been taken in for questioning and had been warned about staying away from us. We'd filed for a restraining order, but I doubted a piece of paper would keep her away.

For now, I wasn't going to worry about it. I'd decided on a hair-brained scheme to show my woman how much she meant to me, and I'd roped in Avy, Noni, and Rea. Abby had wanted in but wasn't feeling well with the new pregnancy, and I hadn't wanted to add any stress to her. Avy and Noni weren't happy about what I wanted them to do, but Rea, she was excited *'weird woman,'* I thought with a grin as Hawke, and I pulled into the pub. Avy had closed it for an hour between four and five just for me.

Opening the door, we walked in, and I saw that everything was set up for our rehearsal

"I cannot believe I'm doing this for you," Noni scowled at me with her hands on her hips.

"It's not like you're doing it for free," I shot back. "I'm sending you all for a whole weekend at a spa and paying for all your treatments. It probably would have been cheaper to hire professionals."

"There's still time," Avy muttered, nervously wringing her hands. Rea slapped her hands on the bar, standing up from the bar stool she'd been sitting on.

"Relax, ladies, we're just the pretty flowerpots. All we have to do is the shoo-wop thing as backing. We'll be good. I'm looking forward to it," she said, bouncing over to me, batting her lashes as she looked up at me with a wide grin.

"Who knew you'd be so romantic, Rogue," she said teasingly.

Gently I pushed her face away from me. "Give over, woman," I muttered.

"Fine," Noni huffed. "It is pretty romantic, and it's not often I get to see you make an idiot of yourself for a good reason."

She walked over to the karaoke machine, picked up the mics, and handed them out. "So, what are we singing?"

I pulled at my neck, feeling the red creeping up my face from my chest, clearing my throat. I put my hands on my hips, saying a little sheepishly, "I Can't Help Myself by Four Tops. It's her favourite song and says everything I need to say."

Hawke chuckled from where he was sitting at the bar, watching us. Glaring at him, I pointed my finger, "Don't say anything to the others. This is a surprise, and they'll ruin it by spilling the beans."

He motioned like he was zipping his lips, but he was still smirking, "Your secret is safe with me. Just one thing you need to speak to the prospects after church on Saturday because it's meant to be their night," he warned.

I nodded, "Yeah, I will."

Avy called me over, "Right, we have the song up. Let's get rehearsing."

An hour later, we nearly had it down. Another couple of hours, and we'd have it sorted. I wasn't feeling nearly as sick about doing something like this now. The plus was that the girls had fun.

I left them at the pub when Bond came in to ride with me to Julia's parents' home, where her brother, sister-in-law, and nephews now lived.

Pulling up, I got off, turning to Bond, who was still sitting on his bike. "I'm heading into the village for a bit Rogue, text me when you are ready, and I'll head back to ride back with you."

"Cool, brother. Ride safe and keep your head on the swivel," I warned him.

Giving me a chin tilt, he pulled slowly away from the kerb while I went into the house.

Pulling Jules into my arms, I laid a hot hard kiss on her lips, much to her nephews' disgust.

I managed to get Warren out of the house without too much hassle, taking the beer he handed me and settling into one of the patio chairs on their back deck.

Taking a long swig from his bottle, he studied me with dark eyes, patiently waiting.

181

When I didn't say anything, unsure how to bring up what I wanted to discuss, he made it easy for me when he said, "So you're going to marry my sister?"

I grinned in relief at his opening. "Funny you should ask. Can you and Deb make it to the pub on Saturday night?"

"I'm sure we can make a plan. Why?"

I went on to tell him what I had planned. By the time I finished, he was laughing hard. When he finally pulled himself together, wiping the tears of laughter from his eyes, he held out his hand to me.

Taking it, and I shook it.

"Welcome to the family, Rogue. I'm glad she found someone like you. Don't fuck it up."

I shook my head, shrugging, "No plans to, brother, but I'm a dude, and I'm bound to fuck up sometimes, but never in a way that will hurt her."

"Eh, we all fuck up eventually, sometimes intentionally. Makeup sex is explosive." Suddenly he realised what he'd said because he gagged, saying, "But I don't want to know if you do that because you know… she's my sister."

I guffawed at his expression, glad my woman's brother was a good man, not a dick.

Finishing our beers, we went back inside and spent the rest of the evening being entertained by Julia's nephews.

CHAPTER 16

CROW MC CLUBHOUSE

REAPER

The entire MC, including the kids, were told to be in the clubhouse by three o'clock. Most were already there waiting for me to tell them what the meeting was about. We were waiting for my parents and Bren, who they'd gone to collect from a friend's house.

I looked over at Gunny and got a nod when I saw the four boxes sitting at the table next to him.

Hearing a feminine laugh, I looked over at the table where the women were sitting, Abby still with a green tinge to her face. I was worried about my woman and how sick she was at only eight weeks pregnant. It was already taking its toll on her. We'd had to tell the kids sooner than we'd wanted because she was constantly sick. She assured me she'd been sick as a dog with Sam too. Rea was keeping an eye on her. I knew Rogue had something big planned for tonight and wondered if we would make it. I watched as Rea handed her a couple of pills and what looked like ginger ale. Rea looked up and caught me watching them, giving me a wink and a thumbs up before walking back over to Onyx, standing at the bar holding Mila.

I was relieved to see that they were back where they had been years ago and were solid once again. I don't think the women in this family realised how much we depended on them. Yes, we could handle the dirty to make sure they were safe and looked after, but the real strength came in running the day-to-day shit like they did and making it look easy while they did it.

Seeing my dad and mum come through the clubhouse doors with Bren, finally we were all there.

Walking over to where Gunny was sitting, I whistled loudly to get everyone's attention.

"Skinny, Blaze, Bond, and Cairo, get your arses up here. And Cairo, you better have a fucking shirt on by the time you get to me," I bellowed as I saw him walk over to me, his bare chest gleaming under the lights. I don't know why the fucker had an aversion to shirts. I wondered what he was going to do in the winter. I shook my head at him as he grinned unrepentantly at me, his teeth pearly white in his tanned face, before pulling his shirt from where it had been hanging from his back pocket, dragging it over his head, and settling against him before he got to me.

I looked them over as they stood in the at-ease position drilled into us by the military. It seemed you could take the man out of the military but not the military out of the man.

"This is an important day not only for our prospects who have all been voted to become full brothers," I paused as I watched the words I'd just uttered penetrate through to our four prospects. They, as one, started to grin before I continued. "But for all of us. We haven't had any prospects join the Crow MC as full brothers since Rogue, Dragon, Onyx, Draco, and I prospected fourteen years ago. Bull, Navy, and Hawk were lucky enough not to have to go through prospecting.

"Originally, we'd thought we'd make the prospects do six months, but you four came in and didn't hesitate once to do what was asked of you. We decided a few weeks ago that three months would more than suffice. Now that's not to say in the future, prospects won't need to do between six months and a year," I said seriously.

Looking over the crowd, I call out, "Bull, if you could come to stand with Skinny, Rea with Bond, Gunny with Blaze, and Aunt Maggie with Cairo."

Once they were all in position, I handed Bull, Avy, Gunny, and Aunt Maggie a box each.

You could have heard a pin drop as everyone waited. I looked around to see Ben, Sam, and Alec looking on interestedly, hunger in their eyes.

Soon I thought.

Turning back to the four, holding the boxes, I said, "If you four could open those and take out their cuts."

I waited until they each held a brand new cut in their hands before asking the prospect to remove their prospect cuts.

"This is the last time I'll call you this. Prospects, remove your prospect cuts and hand them to Thor."

Looking solemn, they each did this, gently folding them in half and handing them to Thor when he held his hand out for them. They waited for me to continue. "Bull, if you'd like to help Skinny with his new cut, then Rea for Bond, Gunny for Blaze, and Aunt Maggie for Cairo."

Once their new cuts had been settled on their shoulders, everyone could see the pride on their faces as they turned back around to the family smiling wide. There were whistles, claps, and cheers from the rest of the MC, but I wasn't finished yet.

Whistling again, I called for silence, "Shut it, you mangy lot," I yelled out, getting chuckles and laughter back before I could continue.

"Now, you four may wonder why I had these particular members of the MC hand you your new cuts to welcome you to the brotherhood. Bull and Skinny are self-explanatory, being blood brothers. Rea, Gunny, and Aunt Maggie specifically asked if they could be part of your ceremony because each of you has come to mean something to them."

I grinned at the look on Skinny, Blaze, Bond, and Cairo's faces as the realisation of what I'd just said penetrated through to them. Not only were they part of the brotherhood, but they were considered family.

Loudly, I bellowed, "So, with that, let's welcome our new brothers to the brotherhood and family."

Standing tall, I raised my hand loudly, stating, "Brotherhood and Family before all."

A resounding return shout of "Brotherhood and Family before all," accompanied by foot stomping and beating of hands on tables.

Once everyone had settled down, I looked with pride around our clubhouse and everyone in it, I went to each of my new brothers, gripped their hands, and hugged each of them, slapping a hand hard on their backs.

"Welcome, Brothers."

"Pres," Skinny replied, his face for once not in its usual serious expression.

"Pres," Bond acknowledged, blinking hard. Pulling him close, I pressed my forehead to his, my hand hard on his neck. "You good, brother?"

"Yeah, Pres, I just wasn't expecting to find a home like this when I got out." I shook him gently from side to side until I could see he was okay. "Welcome home, Bond." Letting him go, I moved on to Blaze.

"Pres," Blaze said with a wide grin on his face.

"Welcome, Brother."

"Thanks, Pres."

"Pres," Cairo said, returning my back slap, stepping back he said. "Thanks for having me."

I laughed, "You drive me insane, brother, but you're a good one."

Once I was done welcoming them, the rest of the family descended on them, letting them know they were to let loose and enjoy tonight. We'd make sure they got home safe and sound. Liam was going to bring a few of his guys in to watch as security while we were out for the night, and Mum had arranged for one of her friends to come and sit with the kids in the house, not that they needed it, but I knew that the women would feel better having an adult in the house with them.

I noticed that Rogue took each of the new brothers aside and spoke to them. They all nodded and grinned, some of them outright laughing, but not one looked put out that he was going to be stealing their thunder later tonight.

We'd chosen well with this group of prospects. None of us were sure if we wanted to bring in any more or if we would stay as we were. I thought we'd play it by ear for now.

CHAPTER 17

CORVUS PUB
KARAOKE NIGHT
JULY 2003

JULIA

It had been a great afternoon watching the prospects get sworn in as full brothers. Rogue had left me earlier, saying he had to help at the gym but would be back to pick me up for the karaoke evening at the pub to celebrate the new brothers.

I was feeling all kinds of sexy this evening. The Crow women had persuaded me to go shopping for a few outfits, with them saying they would all dress up tonight as part of the celebration for the new MC members. I was in an emerald green rockabilly style dress, cut low, clung to my breasts, nipped in at the waist, and flared out in a full skirt that fell just below my knees. I had on a pair of green and white chunky heeled shoes. After we'd bought our outfits, the girls treated me to having my hair and nails done. My hair was up in victory rolls in the front with a green and white flower pinning them back.

I loved the whole outfit, including the new underwear, garter belt, and stockings I'd invested in. I wondered why I'd never tried this style before. It suited my figure, and I felt both sexy and flirty in it. The best had been Marcus' reaction when I walked downstairs. He hadn't been home when we got back, so I'd gone upstairs to change.

I'd walked down the stairs holding tight to the banister as I wasn't used to wearing heels and had looked up when I heard a low moan.

He was already dressed in dark jeans and a button-up shirt with his boots and looked hot as fuck standing there with his fist pressed to his mouth. He then ran his hands through his hair before walking over to the bottom of the stairs and holding his hand out to me. I took it and walked down the last few stairs as he hungrily eyed me up and down. I'd come to a stop at the step just above where he was standing and looked down into his eyes.

He swallowed and growled out, "Christ baby, you are so fucking sexy. All I want to do is take you upstairs, strip you, and fuck you."

I was squirming by the time he finished his speech. I could feel myself getting wet at the thought of all he would do to me.

He pulled me closer to me and whispered in my ear, "Please tell me you're wearing a garter belt, and my evening will be made."

Smiling widely, I pushed his hand under my skirt so he could feel my stockings and garter belt. He ground his head against my chest, making me giggle as he muttered, "Fucking killing me, baby. I can't wait until we get home tonight. Those rings on our bed need to be used," he muttered on a sigh then he pressed a kiss to my chest just above my breasts, making me shiver in delight.

"If you two are finished eye fucking each other and whispering sweet nothings, can we go?" Draco asked grumpily from the kitchen doorway.

"Jealous, brother?" Rogue grinned widely at Draco before helping me the rest of the way down the stairs, pushing Draco out of the way as we entered the kitchen where everyone was waiting.

Navy's eyes widened as he took in my outfit. "Jesus, Jules. You've always been gorgeous, but woman, tonight you are smoking."

Laughter followed his comment, and I grinned at him. "Thank you, Navy."

"Gunny's right. You need to find yourself your own woman and stop ogling ours," Rogue declared, encircling me with an arm and pulling me back against his chest.

"For fuck's sake, you guys, I'm not ogling your women. It's not my fault you all found yourselves hot women," he grumbled as the tips ears turned a little pink in his embarrassment.

"Aw, shut it, you lot," I said, pulling away from Rogue.

I went to Navy and pressed a kiss to his cheek. "Thank you for complimenting me, Navy. Don't listen to these yahoos. A woman likes to know she looks good."

Not one to be kept down for long, he just grinned down at me before taking me back to Rogue. Pulling out his camera, he had us stand together, declaring that this night needed to be documented by pictures.

After a few posed ones, the others got involved until there were photos of all of us messing around, including one of Rogue being held up by his brother's bridal style.

Once the hilarity had died down, we'd left for the pub, and I was now sitting at a private table with the rest of the MC family. Everyone was in high spirits. The new brothers were getting drunker by the second and were getting lots of attention from the ladies. I couldn't see that any of them would be going home alone tonight. Even Skinny wasn't looking so serious. I was happy for them and that they had finally got their colours. They deserved them.

Seeing Warren and Deb walk in, I stood up and waved to them, and they motioned that they were getting drinks. Giving them a thumbs up. I sat back down and put my hand on Marcus' nervously bouncing knee.

I had no idea what was up with him, but as soon as we'd arrived at the pub, he started to act like a cat on a hot tin roof. Avy, Rea, and Noni weren't faring any better, and I wondered what the hell was going on with them all. It was a surprise to see Abby there. Reaper was keeping her at his side. She was looking a little better but still not her usual bouncy self. Morning sickness was kicking her arse.

Warren and Deb got to the table and greeted everyone. Marcus stood up and motioned to his chair for Deb to take a seat.

"Thanks, Rogue," she smiled at him with a wink.

I was definitely missing something. Marcus bent and pressed a kiss to my cheek, whispering in my ear, "I'll be back soon, beautiful."

Tilting my head back, I looked at his beautiful face and saw he was sweating. Lifting a hand, I laid it on his cheek, "Are you okay, honey?"

He swallowed. "I will be in about ten minutes."

'I hope,' he muttered under his breath before walking away.

Warren clapped him on the shoulder as he walked past on his way to the karaoke DJ.

Avy came out from behind the bar and stopped at our table. Noni and Rea threw back their shots standing, then Noni turned to me and said, "My brother loves you a lot, Jules. And he's lucky we love him."

With that cryptic remark, they left the table and joined Marcus by the DJ.

I look around the table in confusion. All the brothers were grinning wide. Hawk stood up, pulled his chair from the table, and set it in the middle of the pub dance floor in view of the makeshift stage they had set up. Then walking over to me, he held out his hand for me to take. Still confused, I took it, and he pulled me up and led me towards the chair. A ripple of murmurs went around the pub, wondering what was happening. I could feel my face heating when I realised how many eyes were on me.

Hawk bent and whispered in my ear once I was seated. "Relax and enjoy, Jules. Rogue and the girls have worked hard on this surprise. If you wondered how my brother feels about you, this should show you how much you mean to him. We'll all be standing behind you, so don't worry about your back."

Looking over my shoulder, I saw the entire Crow MC lining up behind me as a buffer. Thor squeezed my shoulder, letting me know he was close. Warren and Deb took up a stance at the end of the Crows.

I was so busy wondering what was happening that I wasn't taking notice of Marcus and the girls at the Karaoke DJ until I heard the DJ speak.

"Let's give a big hand of applause to Rogue and the Crowettes."

We all heard Noni groan out loud at that name, making everyone, including the DJ, laugh. Rogue stood at the centre of the stage, holding onto the microphone so tightly his fingers were white. Avy, Noni, and Rea were all holding mics and were standing off to the side.

"Now I think this man has something he wants to say before they entertain us." The DJ continued before he motioned to Marcus.

"Jules, I want you to know I love you, and you're the best thing that could have happened to me. I know this is one of your favourite songs as your dad used to sing it to your mum. It also tells you how I feel about you. I'm hoping we don't butcher it too much," he joked. "I want to say thanks to my sister, Avy, and Rea for doing this with me." Taking a deep breath, he continued. "Well, here goes nothing."

The opening music to I Can't Help Myself by Four Tops came on, and Marcus started singing with the girls doing the backing for him.

He looked so nervous, but after the first couple of lines, he really got into it, and I knew I was grinning wide. The crowd behind us was going wild, clapping and whistling.

My cheeks hurt from how wide I smiled as he danced his way down from the stage. Clicking his fingers and shuffling his way around the dance floor, hamming it up to the guests at the other tables. He danced his way around the pub dance floor, hips gyrating, making a few ladies gasp as he danced up to them before turning away and finally shimmying his way to me, where I was sitting in the middle of the dance floor. Marcus held out his hand, and when I took it, he pulled me up out of the chair, twirling me around until I was dizzy and laughing. I couldn't believe he did that, declaring how he felt in front of everyone.

Just as he finished the last 'Sugar pie, honey bunch. You know I love you. I can't help myself,' he fell to his knees in front of me, holding up a box with a ring.

As the music ended, he asked, "Julia, I love you with all my heart. You keep me grounded. Will you marry me?"

Smiling wide, I could feel the tears as he finished. I cupped his handsome face with the palm of my hand, "I'd love to marry you," I answered.

There were more hoots and hollering as the MC descended on us. Rogue got teased about his singing skills. I hugged the girls and thanked them for helping him make my night. They'd waved it off as if it was nothing, stating that this was what family did even if it was out of their comfort zone.

Warren and Deb pulled me into a hug admiring my ring. I finally had time to study it. It was a beautiful emerald surrounded by a ring of diamonds in white gold.

"Wow, that's gorgeous," Deb gushed, holding my hand up to the light.

Warren just smiled, not looking surprised.

"You knew?" I declared.

"I did," he agreed. "That's what he came to see me about the other night at the house. Marcus said he knew he didn't need it, but as dad was no longer here, he felt it right to ask me."

I blinked rapidly to stop the tears. That Marcus had respected my brother enough to speak to him made my heart swell with love. Just then, I felt an arm curl around my waist, and a kiss pressed to the side of my temple. I relaxed into Marcus. "You good, babe?" Tilting my head to look at him, I nodded, "Yeah, honey, I'm good."

Thor pulled me from Marcus's arms, wrapped me in his arms, and hugged me tight.

"Welcome to the family."

Hugging him back just as tight, "Thank you, Thor," I responded, letting go and smiling happily up at him.

I finally made it around to the new brothers and apologised for hijacking their celebration, but they just waved it off like it wasn't a big deal.

Bond said it was the best way to celebrate becoming brothers because that was what the Crow MC was about. It was about Brotherhood and Family before All.

CHAPTER 18

ROGUE

My proposal had gone down better than expected. For all their teasing, my brothers had each, in their own time, come and congratulated me on being brave enough to do what I'd done. The look of happiness on Julia's face when she realised, was enough for me to do it again and again if I needed to.

My dad had been grinning big when he'd pulled me into a hug.

"Proud of you, son," he said softly in my ear before hugging me again and letting me go.

It seemed that my proposal and choice of music had set off a need to dance, and the karaoke DJ was happy to comply, so instead of karaoke, we now had a disco going.

A familiar arm wrapped around my waist. I knew it wasn't my woman as I was watching her showing off her ring to anyone who asked. Tilting my head down, I looked into the familiar blue eyes of my sister.

"You did good, Marcus," Noni smiled at me.

Even though I knew she was happy for me, I could see the small hint of sadness that always seemed to be in her eyes.

Pressing a kiss to her forehead, I hugged her tight to my side, "Couldn't have done it without you, Noni," I reminded her.

"True," she grinned up at me before continuing. "I had fun, and you don't have to send us to a spa weekend. We were just messing with you."

"I'll still send you all, including Julia, but you'll need to wait until Abby feels better. In fact, why don't you find a spa weekend for around October, arrange it, and let me know how much?" I suggested.

Noni's eyes widened in surprise, "Really, all of us?"

Nodding again, my eyes were fixed on Julia as I watched her animatedly chat with the new brothers, and if I knew her, she was apologising for hi-jacking their night.

A sharp pinch to my stomach made me grunt and turn back to my sister, who was looking at me in amusement.

"What?" I questioned.

"Are you sure you mean all of us? That's going to cost a bomb," she asked.

"Yeah, sis, all of you. You're all worth it," I answered.

"Okay," she agreed, then continued. "I know we don't always see eye to eye Marcus, but I wanted you to know that I love you. I'm proud of you and happy you made it home in one piece."

My throat tightened. My sister and I weren't as close as Reaper and Avy or Draco, Onyx, and Bella. But I loved her nonetheless.

Wrapping her tight in my arms, I squeezed her tight, picking her up before putting her back down. I didn't need to say anything. She knew what I meant. But I said it anyway as I let her go, "Love you to Noni."

Then Avy pulled her onto the dance floor where Rea and Julia were waiting for her. My woman blew me a kiss, her smile lighting up the room, and like a sap, I returned it, not caring about the ribbing I knew I'd be getting from my brothers.

I couldn't wait to get her home and strip her out of her new outfit. I was intrigued by what she had on under her new dress.

A couple of hours later, we poured the drunk prospects into a vehicle, and Bull and Noni took them home.

Soon after I had had a giggling, Julia pressed up against our closed bedroom door. I kissed up her throat to the corner of her mouth, her lips parted under mine, I deepened our kiss as I thrust a thigh between her parted legs. A deep sigh left her lips as she ground down on me with a little whimper. Running my hand from her knee up and under her skirt until I got to the bare skin of her thigh, which I squeezed as I ran my hand higher and around to her backside, still not encountering any underwear. I got hard as I explored further, pulling my lips from hers in stunned surprise when I found no underwear at all.

Her brown eyes opened when my lips didn't return to kissing her.

She was frowning at me. "Why'd you stop?" she grumbled, pulling my head towards her.

I resisted and asked her hoarsely, "Babe, do you have any underwear on?"

She smirked a little naughtily at me. "Nope."

That was me I was done for. I dropped to my knees on the floor in front of her with a whispered *'fuck'* as I pushed up the skirt of her dress with a harshly ordered, "Hold it".

"Holy fuck," I whispered as I looked at what my woman was wearing, a gorgeous lacy black garter belt and stockings with nothing else. I parted her soft folds, the thin line of curls wet with moisture. Unable to help myself, I lifted one of her legs and put it over my shoulder before swirling my tongue around her clit from above me. I heard her head hit the door as she said, "Jesus, Rogue give a girl some warning."

I grinned and went back to what was mine. Julia made me proud that she was mine, not allowing her time to adjust. I loved her until she begged me to stop, her legs shaking with her orgasm. Her shoe dug into my back where it rested as she pulled me tighter to her.

Standing, I shuffled her over to the bed, the ledge for her knees already pulled out. Helping her get situated, I pulled my hard cock out from my jeans and then tossed the skirt of her dress over her back as she knelt on all fours. I took a minute to admire her in her heels, stockings, and garter belt. Julia's gorgeous arse was on display before me. Not waiting a moment longer, I thrust my cock hard into her. She took me, pushing back against my pelvis. I couldn't stop. I pounded into her as hard as I could, gripping her hips so hard I knew I'd leave bruises on her. Her ring flashed when she fisted her hands in our sheets as I thrust into her, and I swore that I grew harder, knowing she was mine. I'd never felt this possessiveness for anyone other than her. I felt the familiar tingle starting at the base of my spine, and I thrust hard one more time before I came. After a while, I realised I was lying heavily against Julia and went to stand up, "Sorry, beautiful."

She smiled softly at me, her eyes hazy from pleasure, "I guess you liked the underwear, huh?" she said with a small giggle.

I grinned at her before gently disengaging. Bending, I pulled out the drawer where I kept the cleaning clothes, among other things. Leaning down, I bit gently into the globe in front of me,

"Like is not the word I'd use, sweetheart, more like love. Imagining what you had on under that hot as fuck dress has kept me hard all evening."

I finished cleaning her up before helping her from the bed, out of her clothes, and into the shower.

We weren't in any hurry, and now that we'd got the hard and fast out the way, I was looking forward to some soft and sweet loving from my woman.

It had been a good night, even if I never lived down my proposal. For me, it was enough that Julia knew I'd do anything for her, even make a fool out of myself. I wrapped my arm around her waist and tucked her tight against me as I listened to her breathing deepen as she fell asleep.

A few nights ago, she'd told me why she'd opted to not have children, and I understood it. I didn't like how much pain she'd been in, and I knew the decision had been hard for her. But I felt she'd made the right choice. As I'd explained to her previously, there was no shortage of children to spoil between her brother and my brothers. If she ever wanted to adopt, that would be fine with me.

Now all I had to do was hurry her up and get her down the aisle as fast as I could.

CHAPTER 19

It was Thursday and the last day of school before the summer holidays, and I couldn't wait for a break. The fair was this weekend, and for the previous week, the whole MC, the O'Sheas, and Molly had been working nonstop to get everything ready. It looked to be a good day, raising money for good causes.

The weekend of our engagement was only made better by the news we got from Gary, our local friendly police officer, that Elizabeth had been assessed and sectioned under Section 3 of the Mental Health Act and would be treated under a local mental health hospital for six months after that, she would be assessed again. With her previous history of mental health issues, the case had been fast-tracked.

I breathed a sigh of relief on hearing that and hoped she'd get the treatment needed to make her healthy. I was just glad she'd been sent to a facility far from us and that our lives were back to semi-normal.

I was still a little stunned every time I saw the ring on my finger. I also couldn't help but smile when I remembered how hard Marcus had taken me when we got home. Since then, I'd changed a few of my outfits for when we went out, even going as far as wearing stockings with jeans when we went out last weekend to check out the newly refurbed club. We'd gone on the bike, so I couldn't wear a skirt. We'd been about three hours into the evening when I'd whispered what I was wearing under my jeans to Marcus. I'd squeaked in surprise when he'd pulled me out of my chair and hustled me to Johnny's office, where he'd proceeded to kick him out, bent me over the desk, roughly pulled my jeans down, and proceeded to fuck me so hard I was feeling it for days.

I'd blushed hard when we left the office to find Johnny leaning against the wall, his arms crossed, brow raised in amusement, and a smirk on his lips.

"Have fun?" he queried.

I grinned impishly at him and replied, "Always do," before I'd sashayed away to his and Rogue's laughter. But not before hearing him say to Rogue, "You lucky fucker. You'd better have cleaned up any mess you made."

"No need, brother, she's still wearing all of me."

I'd blushed bright red at the last comment and had ducked into the nearest ladies to clean up. Only to find Noni, Avy, Rea, and Abby feeling better now that her morning sickness had passed, in there. They took one look at my face and snorted hard with laughter.

"You go, girl," Rea said, holding up her hand for a high five. I'd slapped her hand before ducking into a stall. My cheeks were on fire, but I felt a little proud that I'd ventured so far out of my comfort zone. And it was all down to the man watching me with a huge smile as I walked towards him. I sighed in happiness as he took my hand and pulled me down to sit on the chair beside him.

We spent a fantastic evening being shown all the upgrades that had been done and the changes that had been made. This club differed from the rest because the O'Shea's, with the blessing from the club, had changed it from a nightclub to a lounge bar with live music. It was beautifully done in black, silver, and purple, with mood lighting. It had a classy upmarket look to it with big comfortable armchairs, small side tables, and sofas set around what would have been the original dance floor.

They'd built a smaller dance floor, and a slightly raised stage for the live entertainment. The staff behind the bar wore black trousers and black button-down shirts with a purple bow tie, and the serving staff wore black trousers, purple shirts, and black waistcoats.

There would also be a dress code, and while we were wearing jeans tonight, it would be the last time as this was an invitation-only event. The opening night was set for the Saturday the week after the fair, and we'd all be attending that. We women already had our outfits picked out.

Johnny had also set up an agreement with the restaurant next door that anyone they sent over with a specifically stamped token would get ten per cent off their first round of drinks. I hoped it worked out for them. I had a feeling it would because I knew from experience that sometimes after dinner, you weren't ready to go home. To be able to go somewhere like this afterwards where you could relax with a drink, conversation, and live music would be great.

It had been a good night.

I was pulled from my thoughts by the last bell ringing and my kids cheering, making me grin happily.

"Right, you lot, remember this Saturday is the fair at Raven Farm. For those who have volunteered, make sure you are there by 9 a.m. to help finish setting up. Other than that, have a fantastic summer holiday, and I'll see you back here in September. Off you go."

I shooed them out the door, and they hurried off, pushing and shoving as they headed out the door.

I grinned as I packed up the last of my stuff in my rolling trolley. I had two boxes of gifts that I'd have to come back for. For now, I hurried after them to meet the rest of the Crow kids. Only to stop in the hallway outside my class to find them all there.

"What's up?" I asked.

"Nothing," Sam answered. "We thought we'd check on you and see if you need any help to get everything to the car. We saw how many gifts you had piled up when we were in your class earlier."

I smiled at the kids, "Thanks, lads. There are two other boxes in there if you want to grab them for me. I'd appreciate it, so I don't have to come back later. I'm so ready to go home."

Ben and Alec nodded, heading into my classroom. Once they had the boxes, Sam grabbed my trolley handle from me, and the three of them headed off in front of us. Leaving me with Bren, Carly, and Bella.

Shaking my head in amusement, I tilted my head to look at Bella and Carly and noticed all the writing and signatures on their shirts. "Last day for you two. How are you feeling?"

Bella shrugged. "Okay, I'm looking forward to college and getting on with the rest of my life."

Carly nodded in agreement, "Yeah, me too. I'm going to be working full time at the gym. Dragon has me enrolled in a few classes to get my qualifications to hold classes and teach self-defence. I'm happy. School has never been my thing. Bren has some ideas on what we can use the empty shop for next door. We're busy putting together a business plan for Bella to take to the next meeting."

I looked at the shy beauty walking quietly next to me. "Is that right, Bren?"
She nodded her head. I wrapped my arm around her shoulders and squeezed her tightly, "Well then, I'm looking forward to seeing your plans. I know you, so they'll be well thought out."

Bren smiled shyly up at me before telling me, "Bev knows, and so does Momma A, but nobody else. They think it's a great idea, and if the MC agrees, then Bev will run it, and I'll work there after school and on Saturdays."

"But you're still going to find time to train Bren," Carly informed her. "I know you hate it, but it's for your own good."

Bren smiled at her friend, "I'll still train, Carly, don't worry, I'm just going to change my times and come with the boys in the morning."

I admired these kids and the dedication they had to their training and now running businesses.

I wished other kids in the school thought like them, but I knew the Crow kids' way of thinking had to do with their family and the support they received.

I wondered if I could start something in the new year on a volunteer basis, teaching basics like budgeting and finance. I'd think about it and have a chat with the head teacher during the coming months.

We walked out into the bright sunshine, and the heat of the day hit us like a slap in the face. Summer had arrived. I thought it was meant to be thirty five degrees Celsius today, and it certainly felt like it was, as I immediately started sweating.

Ellie was waiting at my car with Abby and was bouncing on her toes, looking like she was going to burst. As soon as she saw us, she ran up shouting, "Guess what?" Not waiting for us to guess, she carried on, "We're going to the beach to celebrate the last day of school." She squealed, clapping her hands happily.

You couldn't help but smile in Ellie's presence. She was a happy kid who loved hard and was always smiling. No one ever had to guess how she felt because she wore her feelings out there for the world to see.

We all grinned at her exuberance, "Well then," I said. "Let's get going. We can't keep the beach waiting."

We'd known that we'd be heading to the beach after school. It had been planned when Ellie had gone to bed, so all we had to do was go home and get changed before we headed out.

An hour later, I was smiling as Marcus pulled his bike into the car park at Bournemouth beach, where I'd first met him just over three months ago. Getting off his bike, I stood next to him as I took my helmet off and handed it to him, still smiling.

"What?" he asked when he saw my smile.

"I was just thinking that this is where we met just over three months ago and how my life has changed since then."

Still sitting on his bike, he wrapped an arm around my waist and pulled me to straddle his thigh.

"All good thoughts, I hope?"

Leaning forward, I pressed my lips to his and whispered, "All happy thoughts, my love."

"Good," he replied, taking my mouth in a hard kiss, releasing my lips when Draco clapped a hand on his shoulder.

"Come on, brother. You can maul your lady later."

I grinned at Draco from across Marcus' body, still held in his arm,

"Jealous Draco?"

"Fuck yeah," he said surprisingly. "I'd like nothing more than to have my woman on the back of my bike and kissing me like you kiss Rogue."

"Maybe stop irritating her then," I said gently.

"But it's so much fun when she explodes," he replied with an unrepentant grin as he got off his bike and started stripping off his leathers.

Rogue's big body shook with laughter at Draco's comment, and I shook my head in amusement. We stripped off our leathers and put them in the saddle bags. I wrapped a sarong around my waist and shoved my feet into flip-flops. Marcus took my hand, and we headed to the rest of the family that had taken up most of the left side of the beach. Setting our stuff down, we headed to the sea and joined the teenagers, Ellie, Rea, and Onyx, who held Mila's hands as she squealed every time the sea rushed over her feet, making us laugh.

We had a good day. Kate and Maggie had packed up a feast for us, so there was no need to head home early. We finally packed up and left at eight o'clock. We all knew we'd have a busy day tomorrow to finish setting everything up before Saturday. The fair was set to run for two days, closing at four on Sunday afternoon.

Avy had also arranged for a couple of bands she knew would play live on Saturday evening. I knew the whole village was looking forward to it. As were the towns in the next county. We'd advertised everywhere, and the pre-booked tickets had sold like hotcakes, so I knew we would be busy, which was good as all the money raised was going to good causes.

CHAPTER 20

ROGUE

Reaper, myself, Draco, and the rest of my brothers were standing around in a loose circle in the field next to Molly's five acres, looking across it at the complete and utter change it had gone through. It looked like an entire town had sprung up. Marquees and gazebos spanned the length and breadth of the field. In the distance, we could just make out Molly's house.

Every shop from our high street was here, we also had an ice cream van, and Noni and Aunt Maggie had a massive catering tent up alongside Avy and Molly's beer tent.

I couldn't believe it was only seven in the morning with the number of people already here bustling around. It was already hot and was expected to get even hotter during the course of the day.

We'd not gone to the gym that morning as everything in the village was closed, with notices telling them to make their way to the field.

Aunt Maggie and Aunt Kate were handing out orders like drill sergeants. I guess that was where Reaper got his bossiness from, his mother, who was a natural at making sure the troops knew what they were doing.

We were standing there waiting to get ours from her. Julia was over at the catering tent with Noni, helping her get all the food set up for the day.

Rea was setting up the first aid tent with the help of the paramedics that came with the ambulance. We'd be getting a fire engine later in the day for the kids to have a look at.

The gazebo for Julia's school had already been set up and was ready to go with all the face paints and glitter tattoos. I knew a long line of children would be at her stall over the next few days.

She never mentioned children, but sometimes I saw her watching Mila, and I could see that it hurt her not to be able to have children of her own. We'd discussed a few options, but for now, we would just spoil the ones in our family. Maybe one day I'd be able to give her that.

Aunt Kate came barrelling down towards us, and we all stood to attention, waiting to get our orders. I could see Shep smirking from where he was standing with my dad, Dog, and Gunny, at the catering tent with cups of coffee in their hands. They knew exactly what she was like having lived with her for so many years.

"Right, you lot," Aunt Kate said, coming to a stop by us. "Head out to where the cars will get parked and make sure everything is set up and marked out. Make sure it's clear which of the parking spaces are for visitors and which are for vendors, as some vendors will be coming and going during the day if they need more stock.

"Pretty soon, we'll have all the school kids arriving that are going to help today. Ben, Sam, and Alec already have the list of who's doing what and at what time, so they all have a chance to have a break. You guys need to sort out which adults will be with which kids at what time."

Aunt Kate started to hand out reams of paper with names and times to Reaper. "Sort it out amongst yourselves," she said before turning on her heel and walking away.

Reaper just shook his head at how his mother was issuing her orders and expected us to do it.

"Man," Hawk whistled. "Your mother must have been hell on wheels when she was younger. Now I know where Avy gets her bossiness from sometimes. She's just nicer about it."

He wasn't wrong. Avy, for all her being quiet and shy, had a steel backbone.

Reaper was reading through all the notes that were on the paper.

Finally, he looked up and said to Sam, Ben, and Alec. "Right, lads, you know which of these kids need more supervision than others. Tell us who needs to go with which kids, and we'll sort it from there."

Sam took the list from him and skimmed through it before marking it off and then allocating our names to whichever group of lads he thought would benefit from us.

By eleven in the morning, the car park was filling up hard and fast. It looked like it was going to be a busy day, and we were going to raise some much-needed cash to get this village back up and running like it used to be.

Navy headed over to tell me and the two lads that had been helping me that it was time for a break. I headed up towards where I knew my woman would be supervising the kids from her school.

When I got there, I saw a queue of about twenty deep waiting for her and the girls helping her, including Bella, Bren, and Carly. Going to Julia, I wrapped an arm around her waist and pressed a kiss to her temple before asking them if anybody wanted anything to drink.

"Yes, please," they all shouted.

"I'm parched," Bella said, pushing back a lock of hair that had fallen across her forehead and tucking it behind her ear.

All the way on my walk to the tent, I'd had a feeling like someone was watching me. The feeling of being watched had started yesterday and hadn't eased off.

Scanning the tents and gazebos around me, I noticed three lads were watching the girls. They all looked related with the same black hair, tanned skin, and lanky build. They looked like they ranged from about fifteen to eighteen. When Julia saw what I was looking at with narrowed eyes, she just smiled and said, "It's just innocent, babe, the girls are gorgeous, and they're going to get lots of attention. You guys are just going to have to get used to it."

"No, we bloody don't," I retorted with a grumble. "It's bad enough worrying about the lads and what they're getting into, never mind having lads around our girls."

Julia threw back her head and laughed loudly at my moaning. The girls joined in. I hadn't realised they'd been listening to me.

With a small deprecating smile, Carly said, "You don't have to worry about me, Rogue. It's only Bella and Bren that you really have to worry about. I promise you they are more than capable of looking after themselves."

I narrowed my eyes at Carly at her comment. She'd better not be thinking she wasn't as important to us as much as Bren and Bella were.

"What do you mean it's only Bella and Bren that need worrying about," I asked.

She shrugged her shoulders, answering with her eyes slightly lowered.

"Lads aren't interested in me. They all think I'm too muscular and look like a boy."

Behind her, Bren and Bella looked pissed on her behalf.

"I mean, I get it," Carly continued. "I don't know anything about make-up or how to dress like a girl. I'm in the gym all the time, so shorts and tracksuits are my norm. Until I met Bella and Bren, I didn't mix with other girls because we had nothing in common. I am muscular because of my work, and there is no way I'm stopping doing it."

"Well, that's a relief that you like your job," I replied. "Dragon and I would be lost without you, girl. You run the gym like a well-oiled machine. I'm happy you'll be there almost full time from September."

I could see that Julia wasn't happy with how Carly saw herself. Neither was I, but I didn't want to make her more uncomfortable. It had to be really bothering her, and I wondered if someone had said something.

Bren and Bella looked at her and disagreed, "That's not right, Carly, you're beautiful," Bella told her.

"And if lads don't see that, then it's their loss, not yours. If they're not man enough to be happy that you can look after yourself, then they're not for you," Bren agreed.

"Well, as far as I'm concerned, you're all beautiful, and none of you is dating until you are thirty-five. None of us would be able to take it," I informed them with a smile.

They all chuckled, not believing me, "I'm telling you, just you wait until some scrawny lad comes to try to pick one of you up from our house. They'll have to run the gauntlet. Don't think they're just going to be able to rock up and take you out without going through all of us first, never mind Sam, Alec, and Ben. There's no way Ben will let anybody take Bren out without first knowing everything about them, and you haven't taken Reaper into account."

Julia just shook her head at me in amusement. "Don't worry, girls, when the time comes, us women will run interference for you."

I snorted and smiled at my woman, hugging her to my side. I knew she'd be working on Carly about her self-esteem. She had the experience of having been there herself.

Dropping a kiss on her forehead, I left them to go and get some drinks, knowing I'd be back before long. But not before stopping in front of the lads watching the girls, looking at them with a raised brow, I ask, "All right, lads."

They grinned at me, not in the least concerned that they'd been caught, before nodding at me and moving on.

I heard a stern, "Rogue," from behind me.

Turning, I saw Julia standing, glaring at me with her hands on her hips.

I winked and grinned at her unrepentantly, then went to get drinks for her and the girls.

Did I care that I'd probably scared the piss out of the lads? Fuck no. I was them once, and I knew what they'd thought while they watched the girls.

Horny little fuckers, needed to find other girls to pay attention to. Maybe it's just as well Julia and I can't have kids. I'd probably end up doing time if we had girls.

Heading into the catering tent, I let out a sigh of relief to be out of the unrelenting sun. Heading to the pub side, I went behind the bar and picked up a pack of ten bottles of water.

"Who's that for?" Avy asked.

"Julia and the girls, they've run out and are slammed, so they can't come and get it themselves," I replied, taking a tenner out of my pocket and putting it in the kitty.

"You don't have to pay Rogue," Avy said, making as if to take the money out.

I stopped her, "It's for a good cause, Avs, leave it."

"Okay," she agreed with a smile as Alec and Ben walked up to the bar.

"What can I get you, lads?" she asked them.

"Just a coke, please, Avy," Ben said.

"Same for me, and can I get one for Sam, please," Alec requested.

Avy left to get their drinks, and I looked up to see the lads I'd seen watching our girls earlier now sitting at a table eating lunch.

"Who are those lads," I questioned our boys, nodding towards them.

Sam and Alec turned to look before turning back to me. "They're the Temple brothers. Why?"

I shrugged my shoulders, still watching them. The oldest looked up, catching me. He gave me a nod when he saw me talking to Sam and Alec.

"They were watching the girls," I answered.

Straight away, Ben tensed. I clapped his shoulder. "They didn't do anything, Ben. I just want to know more about them."

Ben relaxed slightly and surprisingly said, "They're actually nice guys, normal family. They have two older sisters that they love and treat with respect. If you met their dad, you'd get it. He treats their mum like a queen. They moved from the estate about four years ago into a nice house in a better area. I hate to say it, but when Bren is older and if one of them wanted to take her out, I would have a hard time saying no."

"Huh," I say, surprised.

"Yeah," Alec agreed with a nod. "They're solid lads."

"Okay, then," I said as Avy came back with the boys' cokes filled with ice and handed them over.

As we left the tent, I stopped at the table with the Temple boys.

"Lads," I greeted them.

"Sir." I got a nod from all three of them.

Turning to Ben, I told him and Alec, "Take this to Jules and the girls for me, please. I'll be there in a few." I handed over the bottles of water.

Ben nodded, taking the water from me before greeting the lads sitting at the table with a smile, "Beau, Booker, Brice."

They returned the greeting, and Alec and Ben took off.

Holding my hand out to the oldest of the three, I introduced myself.

"Name's Rogue. I'm guessing you're Beau? Tell me why you were watching our girls?"

Smiling, Beau shook my hand before introducing me to his brothers, "These are my twin brothers, Booker and Brice."

I shook hands with the other brothers. They weren't identical, but they were pretty close to it.

"We weren't watching the girls in a way that you need to be worried about. Granted, they are all beautiful, but we're more interested in their brains than their looks. We especially are not looking at Bren that way. She is way too young," Beau continued.

I raised my eyebrows at his comment. "Explain?"

Beau looked at his brothers, and they had silent communication going on between them.

"We know we can't prospect yet because we need to finish school first. I'm eighteen and in college, and my brothers will be in college next September. They're sixteen." Beau

244

continued. "I've been playing the stock market for a while now. It's how we got out of the estate. I've been told about some stock, but I don't think my information is correct, and I want to check with Bella to see if she knows anything before I touch it. I'm good, but she is better than me. We were just waiting for there to be a break in their queue so I could approach her. They know us and know we respect women. My dad would kick our butts if we didn't, and then our sisters and mum would.

"Plus, everyone knows Sam has a thing for Bella, but she thinks he's too young. And Ben is protective over his sisters with good cause, plus Bren is only twelve, so we get it. The only one we don't really know is Carly."

"That's all?" I questioned, not wanting to think about what they had just said about Sam and Bella.

They all nodded before Booker said, "That, and we'd like to make it known we'd like to prospect when the time is right."

I eyed them all, seeing no deceit in their eyes. I nodded, tapping on the table with my hand. I stood and told them, "Okay, if you are serious, be at the manor on Sunday evening. We'll be having a barbecue when this is all done. You can speak to Bella and let Reaper know about wanting to prospect."

"We'll be there," Beau agreed.

Turning, I left them to check in on the girls. Seeing they weren't as busy, I let Bella know about Beau, and she nodded and agreed to see him. After kissing my woman, I left them to it, but as I wend my way back to the car park and duties, the hair on the back of my neck stood up, and I again felt like I was being watched. Stopping in the shade of a gazebo, I slowly ran my eyes around but couldn't see anything or anyone that looked out of place.

I still mentioned it to my brothers when I got back to them. Having been in the military as long as we all had, we learned to trust our guts, and mine was telling me something was coming.

CHAPTER 21

ELIZABETH

I watched from the shadow of a gazebo as Rogue stopped and scanned the crowds. I'd been following him all morning.

They thought they were safe because I should be locked in a room in a ward with no way out. But I was good at getting out of places I didn't want to be.

None of this would be a problem if he'd just picked me. I knew we had a connection. We always had. I knew it from when he helped me up off the floor when I'd fallen in Year 10 at school. He'd made sure I was okay, taken me to the nurse, and then left me there.

I'd tried everything to get his attention, but he ignored me. Nobody ignored me. Just ask my stupid sister, the perfect one. Not so perfect when they pulled her out of the river days later. Nobody believed the person who said they'd seen me push her. All it took was big crocodile tears, and that was that.

Then there was the parasite that took over my body for way too long and still didn't die when I threw myself down the stairs. Pity her father came home when he did, or she'd be no more too.

Now all I had to do was get Rogue by himself, and he'd see. He was meant to be mine, and if he disagreed, then I'll just kill Julia. Not like anybody would miss the big fat lump.

I giggled a little at the thought of cutting into her and making her bleed, or maybe I'd cut into Rogue for not seeing me. Whichever I got to first would feel the blade of my knife.

I ran my finger over the blade in my bag a few times until I felt that delicious pain as it cut into me. Bringing my bleeding finger to my lips, I sucked on it until the bleeding stopped.

Yes, someone would be feeling my blade before long.

Leaving the fair, I needed to find somewhere to lie low and make plans.

CHAPTER 22

JULIA

I'd woken up early that morning and decided to surprise my man by waking him up in the best way possible. It hadn't taken long before he took charge, and we both left our room with a happy glow.

Reaper had called Church for that evening to discuss the fair that had finished yesterday. It had been a fantastic weekend, and we were all still buzzing from the amazing turnout and the support shown to our little village.

Walking into the kitchen together, it was to see a bunch of bleary-eyed teenage boys sitting around the kitchen table, waiting for a lift to the gym. We seemed to have collected another three over the weekend.

I'd heard Reaper on the phone last night with their parents, ensuring that it was okay for them to stay with us.

They'd been having a good time at the barbecue we'd had after the fair, and Sam had invited them to stay the night. Bella and Beau had had their heads together over a computer for most of the evening. And by the end, they'd seemed to have made a decision. I didn't understand half of what they'd been talking about, but they'd pulled Avy and Skinny into the conversation, and the four of them had agreed on whatever it was that was bothering Beau.

I knew all three lads. They'd each made their way through my class over the years. I liked them all and their parents.

Yawning, I headed to the coffee pot, patting Brice on the shoulder as I went past. He was the quietest of the three brothers, and I wasn't ashamed to say he'd been my favourite.

"Ms Julia," they all said, and I waved my hand at them. Pouring a mug, I turned to them after taking a sip and saying, "Just

Julia, lads. You've all finished school, and if you're going to be spending time here, then Julia is fine with me."

Getting nods and smiles back, I watched as everyone gathered their gym bags before offering to drive if they needed an extra car.

Bren came stumbling through the doors with Bella and Carly and hearing my offer, they took me up on it.

Beau and his brothers went to Beau's car, an old Vauxhall I knew his oldest sister used to drive. Carly stopped in front of their vehicle, wrapping her hand tight around the handle of her bag.

"Do you want to come to the gym with us this morning? If you are going to be joining the MC, then you need to start training with us," she informed them.

Surprisingly, Brice answered, his eyes never leaving Carly's face, "We'll be there. We need to go home and get clothing first," he agreed.

Carly nodded, turning and taking a deep breath as she walked over to me, her hands shaking. Smiling, I squeezed her hand as she walked past. I knew it had taken courage for her to speak to the lads. She was so confident in what she did and how she taught that it was always a bit of a surprise when she came over as unsure.

Getting into my car, I pulled out behind Reaper, Draco, Dragon, and Rogue. Behind me was Navy with our lads, then Beau and his brothers, followed by the rest of the MC.

It always caused a bit of a thrill to run through me at the sound of their bikes rumbling down the road.

The drive seemed to fly by as I listened to the girls' chatter. I'd thought I'd get out of a gym session that morning, but Carly was having none of it. Luckily, I kept my gym bag in the car. Grabbing it, I hurried in after them to get changed.

An hour later, I felt like I was dying. I was laid back on the mats, a sweating, panting mess.

"Not sure what I've done to upset you, Carly, but I think you're trying to kill me," I wheezed when she stopped by to check on me.

She laughed out loud before collecting herself, grinning down at me before replying, "I don't hate you. Your old routine was getting too easy for you, so I mixed it up a little. Have you done your cool down?"

"Yes, you slave driver, I've done it all. Just leave me here to die," I groaned dramatically, throwing an arm over my face.

There was a smattering of deep chuckles from around me, and I was well aware everyone was laughing at me. I didn't care. The girl had killed me.

"Babe," I heard Marcus say, his voice filled with amusement. Lifting my arm off my face, I tilted my head back to look at him.

His face was filled with laughter as he looked down at me.

"We'll have to move here, Marcus. You'll just have to get used to sleeping at the gym. I don't think I can move," I moaned pitifully.

"I didn't take you for a drama queen, Jules," Dragon said, grinning at me from where he was helping Brice with weights. I saluted him with my middle finger for that remark, causing more amusement to rumble around the gym.

Marcus held out his hand to me to pull me up, muttering and groaning. I took it, and he pulled me to a standing position. Pressing a kiss to my lips, he hugged me, not caring that I was wet with sweat.

"Reaper has asked if Navy and I can go and give Liam a hand with setting up some cameras," he told me.

"Okay, no worries. I'm going to shower and head back to the manor. Stay safe," I replied.

"Yo, Rogue leave the poor woman alone, and let's go," Navy shouted from the door.

I snickered. That man just can't read a room.

Marcus shook his head and waved a hand, "Yeah, yeah."

He gave me another hug and kiss before heading towards his brother.

I laughed when he smacked Navy on the back of the head when he got to him.

The two of them left, still jostling and shoving each other. Shaking my head, I muttered, "Boys are the same no matter the age."

Bren and Bella were already in the changing rooms when I got there.

"Can we catch a lift back to the manor with you?" Bella asked.

"Of course," I replied. "Let me get finished, and then I'll treat you girls to breakfast before we head home."

"Thanks," Bren said with a smile lighting up her face.

I made short work of getting ready, and before long, I was sitting opposite two of the nicest teenagers I'd ever come across, having a fantastic breakfast and enjoying their company.

CHAPTER 23

ROGUE

I was still grinning in amusement at Julia's dramatics when we pulled into the back car park of the newly outfitted lounge bar. I knew they would do well with this one. It was very classy.

Liam, Johnny, and Adam were waiting for us at the back door. Navy and I backed our bikes into a parking lot and got off, taking our helmets with us.

"Hey, thanks for coming," Liam called out in greeting.

"Liam," I acknowledged shaking his hand before greeting Johnny and Adam.

"What do you boys need a hand with?" I inquired, following them down the passage and into the bar area.

Adam pointed to the pile of boxes holding cameras and wiring for CCTV.

I rubbed my hand back and forth over my head when I saw it all laid out.

It's going to be a long day.

"We didn't want the staff to be aware of some of the cameras. There is still something not quite right here," Adam explained. "Johnny and Liam don't know enough about setting them up, which is why I called Reaper for help."

"Okay then, let's get cracking," Navy said, unboxing the goods with Liam. Adam and I went through the plans he had drawn up and started allocating jobs.

As Navy, Adam, and I had the most experience setting up cameras, Liam and Johnny became our gophers fetching and carrying.

It took most of the morning to fit all the inside cameras. After a quick break for lunch, we then started on the outside.

It was late in the day, and I was outside on a ladder, sweating my bollocks off in the sun, fitting the last of the cameras to the outside of the back parking lot. I dipped my hand into my pocket for another screw and came up empty.

"Fuck," I cursed.

I wanted this done and a nice cold drink.

I started down the ladder, and I was near the bottom when something heavy hit the back of my head, and I fell the last few rungs to the ground. Dazed, I look up into the crazy eyes of Elizabeth.

"Night, night," she said, grinning maniacally at me before hitting me again.

Then there was nothing but blackness.

CHAPTER 24

REAPER

Dragon, Draco, and I had just got home and parked when my phone rang.

I just knew in my gut I wouldn't get some time with Abby and that cold beer I'd been looking forward to all day. It was a scorcher of a day.

"Reaper," I answered without looking at the caller ID as I got off my bike.

"Reap, it's Johnny. You guys need to get to the club asap, man. Rogue's gone missing, there's blood on the ground, and the pipe used to hit him."

"What the fuck? When did this happen?"

"About half an hour ago, as far as we can tell, we were finishing up the front and were headed around the back to store the ladders in the shed when we noticed his ladder was still against the wall, but he was gone. As you know, we share the parking with the restaurant next door. Liam is over there asking if we can look at their CCTV as ours wasn't up and running."

"Fuck," I muttered, gritting my teeth. Rogue had mentioned he felt like he was being watched, but none of us could pick up on anything. And we'd kept a careful eye out.

"Johnny, let me tell the brothers, and I'll call you back. If you find anything on the CCTV, call Draco's phone, as my line might be busy."

"Will do, Reaper," he acknowledged before hanging up.

Turning around, I see my brothers waiting for news on what's going on.

"Draco, everyone to Church now, no exceptions. I have to find Julia. I'll fill everyone in as soon as I can."

"Even the kids?"

"Even the kids. Get Skinny and Blaze to lock and arm all the gates. And Draco, I want Molly here too."

He nodded and got on the phone. Dragon jogged off to the security hut, and I knew he'd work on securing the property with the rest of the brothers.

I took off for the house to look for Julia so I could break the news before I told everyone.

I found her in the lounge with Bella, Bren, and Aunt Maggie. They took one look at my face and knew something had happened because they all stood at once.

"Reaper, what's wrong?" Maggie asked.

Going to Julia, I took hold of her hands, and they started to shake. I watched as she straightened her shoulders. She closed her eyes for a second, then opened them, "Who is it?" she asked.

"Rogue's gone missing from the O'Shea club," I answered her.

Her face paled at my words, and I watched as tears filled her eyes, and one dropped onto her cheek. She wiped at it with an impatient hand. I wasn't sure if I expected her to crumble, but I should have known my brother wouldn't have chosen a weak woman.

"Okay then, as there is no body, that means he's still alive. So, what are we doing to find him?" she demanded.

I went to hug her, but she stopped me.

"No hugs. If you hug me, I'll fall apart, and I won't be of any use. Once we've found him, that's another thing. I'll take all the hugs I can get."

I could respect that, so I nodded and told them, "I've called Church. It's mandatory for all kids as well. I've just sent a text to Carly and her grandfather to come in as well. If we need to, we'll take it to the wider village. We'll find him, hun."

Ten minutes later, we are all in the Clubhouse. As there are so many of us with the Mastersons, the Temples, and Liam and Johnny O'Shea, I opted for us all to stay in the main area. Not for the first time, I'm happy that we only allow family and close friends into our sanctuary.

Abby was sitting waiting with our children near the bar, and I headed over to her first, needing to have her in my arms before I told everyone what was going on. Hugging her tight to me, I pressed a kiss to her forehead before turning to the rest of the room to let them know about Rogue being missing.

"I wanted you all here, including the kids, because sometimes they see shit that we as adults miss," I explained.

"It can only be Elizabeth," Dragon stated, "But I thought she was locked away?"

There were loud rumblings of agreement from around the room.

I turned to Skinny, who had been clicking away on his computer at one of the tables. "Anything?"

He held up a finger to me. "One minute, Pres, I'm just making sure of something first."

I nodded as we all waited. I looked around the room and saw Julia standing between Avy and Noni with Bull and Hawk behind them. They each had an arm around her waist, and while Julia was pale, I could see she was determined not to break.

"Got it," Skinny shouted out.

"Let's hear it!"

"Elizabeth Gaines was meant to be put in a maximum security psychiatric hospital, but there seems to be an error on her paperwork, and it shows as minimum security. Looks like this was a simple clerical error that she took advantage of and literally walked out during visiting hours. She's been loose for about five days. Which makes sense as Rogue started to feel like he was being watched on Saturday," Skinny informed us.

"Okay. Skinny, you get pictures of her, and Rogue printed off and hand them out to everyone. Thor, can you call our contact at the police station and let them know what's happened. Cairo, bring the town map and let's get searching and knocking on doors. Bella, Bren, and Carly, if you are going out to help look, make sure you stick with one of the boys. Aunt Maggie, can you and Mum open the cafe and have food ready? I know that as soon as the village finds out, they'll be helping, and we will need them to be fed. Right, let's get a grid search going."

I took the map Cairo handed me and started marking places to search in a grid pattern.

Once I had it all sorted, I straightened.

"Everyone knows what they are doing?" I said to the assembled group.

"Yes, Pres," they shouted back.

"Good. Grab your pictures from Skinny, and let's get our brother back to his Old Lady," I informed the room.

As Skinny started handing out the pictures, I noticed that the Temple lads stopped on their way out the door. They passed the picture amongst themselves.

"You good lads?"

"Yeah, Reaper, but we've seen this woman. She was at the fair this weekend by the tent where the girls were. We thought she was taking a rest in the shade of the tent. Then we saw her again in the parking lot when we were leaving. She was driving a dark brown Ford Transit. I noticed it because one of the brake lights wasn't working," Beau informed me.

"You didn't happen to get the number plate did you?" I queried.

Beau and Booker shook their heads, but Brice answered, "I did."

I breathed a sigh of relief.

"Good lad, give it to Thor, and he'll let the police know so they can issue a BOLO for it."

The three lads did as I asked.

Thank fuck we lived in a small village because I doubted the police in a bigger town would be so helpful.

The tension in my neck was giving me a headache. I pulled on the back of my neck and squeezed. I stopped when soft hands massaged my shoulders, and Abby asked, "What do you need us to do, Kane?"

I look up to see Avy, Noni, Julia, and Molly standing at the table waiting for me.

"Avy, can you and Noni grab your bikes and search the smaller roads in the village? Julia, if you and Molly take one of the Land Rovers, search with that. You are looking for a brown Ford Transit. Thor will give you the registration number. If you find anything, call me, don't go in by yourselves, okay?"

"Okay, Reaper," they acknowledged before dispersing to do as I asked.

Sighing, I pull Abby down onto my lap and bury my head into her neck. The worry about my brother pulling at me. How did we manage to go years in the military with hardly a scratch, only to come home and have him abducted?

"Pops, will Uncle Rogue be okay?" a small voice asked softly. Looking up, I saw our youngest, Ellie. Her little face was pale, and her eyes filled with tears.

"Ah, baby, come here," Abby pulled her onto our laps, and we hugged her tight.

"Your Uncle Rogue is tough," Abby assured her. "Everyone is out looking for him. We'll find him soon."

"Yeah?" Ellie asked, still unsure.

Abby kissed her on the head and cuddled her closer.

"Yeah, sweet girl, we won't stop looking until we find him," I assured her.

My worry was what condition he would be in when we found him.

CHAPTER 25

ROGUE

Waking up slowly, my head pounding in pain. It was like a drum beating in time with every pump of my heart. The last thing I remembered was being up on a ladder helping the O'Sheas fit their security cameras, then nothing but pain as something hit me hard in the back of the head.

I tried to move my arms but couldn't, and as I became more aware, I realised that I was secured to a chair with my arms tied behind me. Pulling slightly at my restraints to test them, I found they were secure.

FUCK.

I kept my head hanging, not wanting to give whoever had taken me a clue that I was awake. While I couldn't hear anything, I couldn't be sure I was alone. Opening my eyes to slits, keeping my head lowered, I scanned the room I was in as much as I could, not seeing or sensing anyone. I lifted my head up to do a better scan and grimaced at the filth of my room.

There was a naked bulb letting off a weak beam of light hanging from the ceiling that had peeling paint. The carpet was filthy, and I could just make out the brown and orange swirl pattern that had been popular in the seventies. There were velvet curtains scattered with moth-eaten holes hanging from a rod on the window. Piles of rubbish and what looked like old needles were piled up in corners of the room, and the door looked like it had been kicked in a few times. It seemed I was in one of the derelict buildings on one of the poorer estates that should have been condemned years ago.

Hearing voices coming closer, I let my head hang again and closed my eyes.

"Jesus, Bets, how hard did you hit him? He should have been awake by now."

It was a man's voice that asked the question.

"Eh, not that hard. Maybe he's just a pussy, not as hard as he'd like us to believe. Not so hard now, are you?"

The voice got closer as someone kicked at one of my legs. I assumed it was Bets.

I ground my teeth, so I didn't make a sound as she kicked me again.

"Stop it," a soft voice said, and I felt a soft cool hand on the back of my neck, "He's still bleeding from where you hit him," the soft voice muttered.

Who the fuck were all these people, I wondered.

"I don't give a fuck," the man muttered, "I want my money, Bets. We helped you get him from the restaurant to here. Now, pay me."

"Jesus, Benji, you and Penny will get your money," Betsy screamed at whoever Benji was.

I opened my eyes slightly and nearly gave myself away to the others when I saw a pair of blue eyes peering at me, they looked vaguely familiar, but I didn't know the face. Her eyes flared briefly when they saw mine, and she put her finger to her lips. Only then did I notice the track marks down her arms and the gauntness of her face, her lips peeling, cracked with small sores around the edges of her mouth and nose. But her eyes were what held me. It took me a while, but I realised that I saw these eyes every day in three children in our home. The woman stood quickly and went to where Bets and what must be Ben's father were standing, screaming at each other.

"I think you hit him too hard, Bets. You've probably cracked his skull. I doubt he will wake up, and I don't want to be found with a body. It was one thing helping you get him here, but I'm not up for murdering him,"

Penny informed Bets, keeping her back to me.

"Oh, for fuck's sake, you and Benji are more useless than tits are to a bull," Bets said, grimacing at the two of them. "I'll show you how dead he is."

From beneath my lashes, I watched her take a knife from the bag she had on her, and she stormed over to me. Pulling my head back, she ran it lightly down the side of my face, it stung as the blood welled and dripped down my neck, but I didn't make a noise or twitch as she waited for some sort of indication to show I was awake.

"Huh? Maybe I did hit him too hard."

She let go of my hair, and I let my head again drop to my chest.

"Well, fuck, it's no fun torturing someone while unconscious," she told me. "I'll leave you for a bit, but I'll be back, handsome. Then you and I can have some fun. Nothing would have happened if you'd chosen me instead of that fat pig," Bets said gleefully before continuing. "Mmh, I can't wait to fuck you. I bet you fuck like a bull," she said as her hand cupped my dick and balls.

They shrivelled at her touch, which made her angrier than she already was. So when Benji again pushed her, she snapped.

I opened my eyes as soon as I felt her move away from me and watched as Benji grabbed hold of Bets shoulders, shaking her and demanding, "Bets, we want the money now."

"You want the money now," Bets screamed at him. I could see Penny cowering at the door. "You want the money now?" Bets screamed at him again. "I'll give you the cocksucking money now," she shrieked before showing her blade right into his heart. Benji's eyes widened in shock, and Penny screamed as Bets threw her head back and laughed as the blood bubbled up as she pulled the knife out before shoving it into him again and then pushing him away to fall to the floor. Rubbing her hands through the blood on his chest, she rubbed her blood-stained hands across her cheeks, smearing the blood all over and then down her arms. Bets looked up as Penny whimpered in the corner, her shocked gaze on Benji lying on the floor.

"You're coming with me," Bets said, pointing her knife at Penny. "I'm not taking any chances that you'll scarper to the cops about this."

With that, she pulled a still whimpering Penny from the room. The last thing I saw was her shocked blue eyes as Bets pulled her from the room by her hair. My gaze returned to Benji lying on the floor.

Not long after, the screaming started coming from a room a bit further along before it was abruptly cut off.

'Cocksucking, bitchcunting, turd burgling fucking whore,' I swore to myself.

This was a fucking mess. I could only hope it didn't take long for everyone to realise I'd been taken. I knew they'd be out looking for me. In the meantime, I'd start trying to work myself free of whatever the fuck they'd tied me up with.

I tried everything I'd been taught to get out of my restraints, but my head was pounding and I was fast fading back to unconsciousness. I hoped I could hold on for as long as it took for my brothers and family to find me. I had a feeling that if they didn't find me soon or if I couldn't free myself, things were only going to get worse for me.

CHAPTER 26

ROGUE

The next time I woke up, the sun was just rising. Benji's body was still on the floor near the door where he'd fallen. The blood was drying in a pool around him, his wide eyes staring at nothing. I started to work on my wrists again and could feel whatever they'd tied me up with starting to cut into my skin, and blood was making my fingers wet. I'd already assessed that there was no way I could break the chair as it was one of the metal framed chairs with a wooden seat that we'd used in school. These things were nearly indestructible.

My head was still throbbing, my vision blurry, and it was taking everything in me not to hurl, not that there would be much in my stomach anyway, not having had anything to eat or drink since yesterday lunchtime.

I could feel myself starting to fade again. The knock on the head was really starting to piss me off.

The next time I woke up, it was to someone shaking my shoulder and whispering, "Hey, you need to wake up so we can get out of here before she wakes up."

Opening my eyes, my vision blurry. All I could see was blonde hair matted with blood. Blinking to clear my vision, I looked at Penny in shock.

"Jesus, sweetheart, what did she do to you?"

Her face was black and blue, and her one eye was so badly damaged I didn't think anything would save the sight in it. Her left ear was bleeding from where it looked like it had been nearly severed from her head. She cradled one arm against her stomach, and I could see all her fingers were broken at strange angles.

In her other hand, she had a knife and awkwardly tried to cut through whatever had me tied to the chair. I could feel the bindings loosen, but not before we heard a screech from down the hallway.

"You fucking cunt, where are you? You'd better not have let my plaything go. Bravo on playing dead. You had me fooled." The voice was getting closer. Penny started to sob slightly as she hacked at my bindings. I was unravelling whatever they'd tied me up with, opening and closing my hands to get feeling back into my hands and arms. I still couldn't stand as my feet were tied to the chair. Penny stood with the hand with the knife hidden behind her as Bets entered the room.

"There you are," Bets said cheerfully, her face breaking into a wide smile as she saw us. She held a knife in her hand different from the one she'd had last night. This one looked like a thin-bladed skinning knife.

"My two playthings together. I think when I'm done with you," she said, turning to Penny and waving her knife through the air at her, "I'm going to find me one of your offspring and play with them. Maybe little Ellie, mmh yeah, Ellie. She won't be so happy and smiley when I'm done with her."

"You leave my children alone," Penny said shakily. "They've been through enough living like we did. They are happy where they are with a good family."

"Oh, that's right, you sold them to the Crows, didn't you? How much were they worth?"

"I didn't sell them. I signed the papers free and clear. I told the lady I spoke to that I didn't want anything for it, just that my kids would go to a good home. Not living with Benji, who would have eventually got them hooked or sold them like he did me," Penny muttered harshly.

She didn't sound good with how her breath rattled in her chest, and I wondered if her ribs had been broken. She was swaying slightly on her feet as she faced off with Betsy.

"Oh, that's right, you and Benji used to be an all-beautiful normal family with jobs and a house on the good side of town until good old Benji got the taste for cocaine and then got you hooked. Forgot all about your precious kids then, didn't you? How the mighty have fallen," she cackled gleefully before suddenly stopping as if a switch had been hit, the smile leaving her face.

"Well, more fool you," Bets continued conversationally, coming closer. "Payment for them would have kept you on drugs for at least a month," she snickered slightly.

"Now, handsome, let's have some fun," Betsy said, smiling at me.

I couldn't help my grimace as I looked at her. I'd seen some gruesome things in my time in the military but nothing like this. She looked like she'd bathed in blood, it was smeared all over her face, and she'd slicked her hair back with it. Her nails and finger beds had dried, black flaking blood embedded in them.

She sauntered over slowly to us, and my hands were screaming in agony. The pins and needles stabbed at me as blood flowed through them.

Penny stepped in front of me, "You don't get to hurt him anymore, Bets. Enough is enough. We're going to leave now."

Brave woman, but I could have told her there was no negotiating with crazy.

Bets snarled in anger before screaming, "You dare to try to stop me, you cunt. I don't think so."

I watched in horror as she lifted her knife over her head and went to bring it down, and I don't know who was more surprised, Bets, Penny, or me when Penny struck before Bets and stabbed the knife she was holding into Bets' stomach before Bets brought her knife down. I could see that it wouldn't slow her down much just because of where it was placed.

Awkwardly standing, I reached over, pulled the knife out of Bets' stomach, and stabbed the knife into her heart. Penny sagged against me as we watched the life drain from Bets' surprised eyes as she fell to the ground. All I felt was relief. My hands were in agony and so swollen I wasn't sure how I'd even held the knife to stab her.

Penny got heavier where she'd been leaning against me, and looking down, I could see the blood bubbling from the side of her mouth.

"Shit," I said, laying her down as gently as I could.

Seeing the knife that Betsy had been holding lying on the floor not too far away. I managed to reach it and cut the duct tape from my legs. Standing up, I hobbled out the door on swollen feet, searching for a phone or some help, whatever I came to first.

Making it to the kitchen, I spied Bets' bag on the table and started rummaging through it, looking for a phone. I found it near the bottom of the bag. Seeing it didn't have much charge left, I decided to call for an ambulance first. I again hobbled outside as I knew they'd need to know where we were. When the emergency operator answered, I told her what we needed and approximately where we were as I recognised the road from when we had ridden down it a few weeks ago. Rea had remarked how odd it was that only one house was left standing when all the others had been knocked down. There was a sign up saying that the new build would be starting in the new year. After giving the emergency services as much information as possible, I headed back to the house to check on Penny.

She was still alive, but I wasn't sure for how much longer. Then, making a decision, I used the last of the battery to call Reaper.

"Reaper, it's me," I told him and stopped him when he started to ask questions, "Brother, I can't talk long as I have a low battery. I've called the emergency services, meet us at the hospital. And I know you won't like this but bring Ben and Bren with you. They need to say bye to their mum. I'll explain everything, but just know she saved me."

With that, the phone died, but I got the message through, and that was all that mattered. Slowly and painfully, I sat down next to her on the filthy floor. I took Penny's uninjured hand and held it as tightly as my swollen fingers would allow. She squeezed mine, and I looked down to see her eyes were open.

"I did the right thing making Benji give up the rights to our kids, didn't I?" she whispered.

"Yeah, babe, you did. They are happy and very loved by all of us. Abby and Reaper are good parents," I assured her.

She closed her eyes for a minute. "Good, they're good kids."

She paused for a minute, and I could hear the breath rattling in her chest and wondered if she would make it to the hospital. She probably shouldn't be talking, but she seemed to want to get things off her chest.

"We weren't always like this," she continued softly. "We had a nice house and good jobs. Then we were invited to a wedding in London for a weekend, and that's where it started. It was meant to be just one time, you know. Before long, we'd lost everything and had to move to the estate when Ben was four and Bren two, and it spiralled from there. I was still sort of managing to make sure they went to school and had food the first couple of years, but after I had Ellie, I gave up."

She falls silent again. I could hear the sirens in the distance and knew it won't be long before they got here.

"Ellie isn't Benji's," Penny continued softly. "He sold me at some party in London. I don't know who her father is. Alec's mum Bev used to go to the same parties. I'm glad she got Alec out when she did. I wish I'd done better."

My heart hurt for this broken woman. I squeezed her hand again before saying, "Shh, sweetheart, the ambulance is nearly here. You need to save your strength for the hospital."

Her eyes opened again, and she smiled sadly at me before saying, "I'm dying. Please let my kids know that I did love them, and I'm sorry for being such a shit mum."

"You can tell them yourself. They'll be at the hospital waiting for you," I informed her just as one of the ambulance crew called out.

I answered, and they came to a stop staring in horror at the carnage in the room. I immediately started talking, so they knew it was safe to come in. They had police with them, as I'd asked for both to be sent.

Some followed us for statements, and others stayed at the site to process it.

This whole situation was a mess and one I wasn't likely to forget anytime soon. I was just pleased to have made it through with minimal damage.

Having seen everything, I had over the years in the military, I'd have thought the depravity of humans wouldn't surprise me anymore. The fact that it had happened in our village and that I'd been the focus of Bets and all the damage she had caused was hard to swallow.

We arrived at the hospital in a short time, and I was happy to see Reaper and Draco waiting for me at the doors. Not that they got to speak to me as the emergency services rushed me past them, but it was enough to know they were there. Now all I needed was Julia, and I'd be good.

CHAPTER 27

JULIA

I sat at the kitchen table the morning after Marcus had been taken with my head in my hands. Marcus had been missing since yesterday afternoon. Everybody had been out looking. Including most of the village, we were all running on fumes. It had been nearly sixteen hours, and we'd found no trace of Elizabeth or the van.

Finally, at four in the morning. Reaper had called everyone in and had them get some sleep. I hadn't been able to. Our bed was too empty and smelt of him. I knew if I stayed there, I'd break, and I wasn't going to break until we found him, alive or dead. So, I'd found myself in the kitchen where I'd been sitting, staring into my cold cup of tea like I'd find some answers there.

"Jules," Dragon said softly.

I looked up to see him framed in the doorway.

His face softened when he looked at me, and I could see he was going to hug me, but I couldn't let him. I held up my hand to stop him.

"Don't hug me, Dragon, not yet. I can't break, and if you hug me, I will. I need to keep going until we find him."

"Okay, babe," Dragon said, nodding before making a cup of coffee and pulling the chair out next to me. "Can I hold your hand, though?"

"Yeah, Dragon, I'd like that."

And that's how we sat until the rest of the house came downstairs, taking comfort from each other.

Once everyone was assembled, Reaper had us break into groups again to start looking. I hoped we'd find him soon. Today I went out with Warren to look, and Debs was helping Maggie and Kate in the cafe with food.

It was close to two in the afternoon when Warren took a call. He was silent as he listened.

Not saying anything, he checked in his mirrors, did an illegal U-turn, and put his foot down.

I grabbed hold of the *oh shit handle* and said, "What the hell Warren? Who was that?"

"It was Draco. They've found him, Jules. He's being taken to the hospital to get checked out. I've been told to get you there as he's asking for you."

My heart skipped a beat at the relief that he'd been found, but in what condition if we had to go to the hospital. I could feel the tears threatening, but I wouldn't allow them to spill until I saw Marcus with my own eyes to assess how he was.

Twenty minutes later, Warren was pulling up at the hospital.

"I'm going to drop you and go and park, Sis. I'll be back as soon as I can. According to Draco, they're in the A&E. Rea has left word to have you sent back."

Nodding, I jumped out of the car and rushed into A & E. I saw almost all the MC was there except some of the women and children. Seeing Draco, I rushed up to him, "Where is he?" I demanded.

"They've taken them back," he answered, taking my arm and getting a nod from the receptionist as she pressed the buzzer to allow us to the back. I knew he couldn't be too bad because they'd not allow us back there if he was.

"Who's them?" I asked as I hurried to follow Draco's long-legged steps.

"Ben, Ellie, and Bren's mum came in with him. She's in a bad way. She was hurt trying to free him."

"Ah, Jesus," I whispered, wondering how she was involved.

And then he was there as Draco pushed open the door to a private room to the side of the A&E, his face pale, wrists bandaged, hands swollen, and a bandage covering his one cheek. Still, other than that, he looked okay.

He opened his eyes and smiled at me as I pushed the door wider to enter the room. I broke as soon as he spoke, "Beautiful, you're a sight for sore eyes."

I couldn't stop the tears as I rushed over to him and pressed my lips gently to his. "Marcus," I whispered against his lips, closing my eyes. I rested my forehead against his shoulder, wetting him with my tears.

"Shh, baby, don't cry," he crooned in my ear, wrapping an arm around me.

I sighed in relief at being in his arms again.

We looked up as the door opened again, and Rea walked in. I saw Draco and Onyx standing in the hallway before the door closed again.

Wiping my hand across my cheeks and drying my tears, I asked Rea, "What's the verdict, Doc?"

She smiled at us before turning to Marcus and saying, "Could be worse, concussion, abrasions, twenty stitches to the laceration at the back of your head, some damage to your hands from being tied up for so long, and severe dehydration. We will keep you in tonight, one because of the concussion but also because we will keep you on intravenous antibiotics for the knife and head wounds. And we'll have to get you some physio for your hands. A nurse will be by shortly to give you a tetanus jab. According to your records, yours is expired."

Marcus grumbled a little at the mention of a jab but didn't say much else, just leant his head back against the pillow for a minute.

Then just as Rea was about to leave the room, he asked, "How's Penny?"

Rea grimaced slightly before replying, "We've made her comfortable. That's all we can really do for now. Abby and Reaper did as you asked and brought in Ben and Bren. It will be a closure for all of them."

Marcus nodded, then winced slightly as the motion must have hurt his head.

"Thanks, Rea. She was courageous towards the end, and I wouldn't be here if it wasn't for her."

Pulling a chair closer to the bed, I sat down as Rea left and gripped Marcus' hand as he fell asleep unwilling to let him go just yet.

Taking my phone from my bag, I sent my brother a message to tell him what was happening and to go home to Deb and the boys.

I then settled in for a long wait as I knew it would take some time before he got taken to a ward, and they kicked me out.

CHAPTER 28

ROGUE

We'd buried Penny a week after I'd been released from the hospital. She had lasted long enough to make her peace with her two older children. Abby hadn't thought it would be good for Ellie to see her as hurt as she was. Penny's body could not cope with the amount of abuse it had been through, and with the drugs, she'd been taking and the damage it had done to her body, she'd had no reserves left to fight. She'd died four hours after we'd arrived.

I'd made sure to tell her children how brave she'd been, and I'd offered to pay for her funeral. We'd buried her in the Crow family plot. When Abby, Reaper, and the kids had gone to clear out their old flat, they'd found a box of pictures and mementoes that showed their parents in a different light before they'd become slaves to the drugs that poisoned them.

It had taken a while, but we were all slowly starting to heal again. We'd all learned something from me being taken. Even with all our training, we weren't invincible. I hadn't been able to free my hands because Benji first cable-tied my wrists, then tied them with curtain tape and wrapped them so many times that there was no way I would have gotten untied.

Reaper had insisted that we rode in pairs from now on, and if we needed to do anything outside of our typical day-to-day lives, we did it in pairs. If we went riding alone, we had to leave the route we were taking and check in every hour.

The O'Sheas carried a lot of guilt as I was taken on their premises. They'd added further cameras and solar panels so they'd have a backup should their electricity be cut.

My recovery had taken some time, and I still had the occasional headache. It was my hands that bothered me. There was some nerve damage from the blood flow being restricted for so long. I'd kept up with my physio to get my grip back as close to where it had been as possible.

As for Julia, she struggled to let me out of her sight, and I understood. We'd only just found each other when I was nearly taken away.

She hadn't wasted any time in marrying me, and two weeks after I was released, the entire family had found themselves at the Registry Office in the village watching us say our vows. We had a catered meal at the pub afterwards. She'd invited the entire village to celebrate with us.

Julia was a gorgeous vision in a cream dress with a lace overlay and a sweetheart neckline. She had on cream heels, her legs bare in favour of our summer heat wave. Her face was alight with laughter as she danced with her brother and laughed at whatever he was saying to her.

While the ladies had all dressed up, we men had been told that black jeans and white dress shirts, along with our cuts, were good enough.

Putting my empty beer down on the bar, I clapped my dad on his shoulder, where he stood next to me, watching the dance floor. He grinned at me, then his eyes drifted to Julia, and he smiled before turning his head to me and saying, "You did good, lad. I'm proud of you."

I cleared the lump out of my throat at the unaccustomed praise from my father.

"Thanks, old man," I grinned at him.

He laughed softly and wrapped his arm around Noni's shoulders when she came and stood between us.

"Happy for you, Marcus," Noni said, smiling up at me.

Returning her smile, I pressed a kiss to her cheek, "Thanks, Sis. Now I'm going to go and take my bride for a spin around the dance floor before we head off on our honeymoon."

I'd booked us two weeks in Tenerife in a private villa, and I was looking forward to having her all to myself.

Julia smiled as she saw me approaching her and Warren over his shoulder.

I tapped him on the shoulder, and he turned with a grin when he saw me and happily handed Julia over to me.

Pulling her in close, I wrapped my arms around her, and she laid her cheek on my chest, her eyes closed and a contented smile on her face.

Yes, it had been a whirlwind couple of months, but I couldn't be happier.

EPILOGUE

JULIA

We'd had some adventures, Rogue and I, travelling every holiday to help my man stay sane. We'd been all over Europe on the bike. Now that was something. I thought I'd never get the feeling back in my arse when we were done. But I enjoyed every minute of it and we saw some beautiful sights.

We were also the favourite aunt and uncle to all the kids, Abby and Reaper had a boy called KJ, and Onyx and Rea had Mila and Bobby. Abby and Rea had given birth within six weeks of each other. It was hard to believe the boys were five already. Plus, there were all the other nieces and nephews that we seemed to have acquired over the years. Because the Crow MC was a prolific lot.

Did I sometimes have a small twinge of envy? Yes, I did, but only sometimes. Marcus and I discussed adopting, but it never seemed like the right time. I always said that when it was meant to happen, it would, and if it didn't, then I was content. But I loved him all the more for wanting to make sure I was happy. And I was.

He still made me feel like the most beautiful woman in the world, and I loved him more than I could say.

We were on the home stretch after spending the October half-term in Cornwall. We'd been all the way down to Land's End and spent a day at a cider farm, where I'd taken lots of information down for Molly, and we'd had some of their products shipped back for everyone to try.

We were only an hour away from home when Marcus put his indicator on to take the next exit off the motorway. I wasn't too surprised. He did this sometimes when we were travelling if he saw something interesting.

Pretty soon, I started seeing signs for Corfe Castle, and I smiled. It seemed my man wasn't ready to go home. Hugging my arms a little tighter around him, he lifted one hand from the bike to squeeze my calf, running his hand up and down it as we slowed to a stop at traffic lights. Lifting up his visor, he smiled at me, his navy eyes happy and relaxed.

"Nearly there," he assured me.

Before long, we were pulling into a hotel. He hadn't spared any expense by the looks of the hotel. It looked like it used to be a manor house, not much different from our home. Stopping the bike, I got off so he could reverse it into a parking space. It was much easier now that I'd had years of practice.

By the time he'd parked, I had my helmet off and was looking around at where we were.

Marcus grabbed our overnight bag from the saddle bags, as I had most of what we needed in my backpack.

He turned to me with a familiar grin. "One more night just you and me, beautiful."

Returning his grin, "Always happy to spend time with you, my love."

Taking my hand, we checked in and were given a key to our room.

I climbed the stairs and looked around at the plush red carpet, chandeliers, and flocked wallpaper. I felt a little underdressed in my bike leathers and dying to soak in a hot bath.

We got to our room, and Marcus unlocked it with an old-fashioned brass key. Walking in, I sucked in my breath at the pure decadence of the room. A massive four-poster bed took up most of the room. The curtains that were draped around it were a deep dark red. Venturing further into the room, I took note of the deep claw-foot bathtub that sat on a raised step to the back of the room. There was a fake wood-burning fire not far from it.

I couldn't wait to sink into that tub in front of the fire and look out at the stars from the large bay window.

"Oh wow, Marcus, this is gorgeous," I whispered in awe as I finished looking around.

Then, hurriedly, I removed my boots and started stripping, only stopping when I heard him chuckle.

"Carry on, beautiful. I'm getting hard just watching you."

Turning slightly, I looked at him over my shoulder to find him leaning back against the door, his arms folded across his chest as he watched me do my impromptu strip tease. I no longer worried about the extra pounds I carried or that my arse jiggled as I walked.

He still made me feel like I was the most beautiful woman in the world.

Grinning at him, I threw my shirt in his face before sauntering towards the bath, leaning forward to start the taps running. Marcus walked behind me as I bent over, his hands hard on my hips. I thrust back against him to find him already hard. Switching the taps off because I knew where this was going and wasn't complaining or stopping it.

"Something I can do for you, Mr Wright?"

"There definitely is Mrs Wright," he replied, his hand already pushing at my leathers to remove them. Before long, we were on the bed, and the bath was forgotten for the moment. It was much later, after opting for room service rather than getting dressed, that I got my bath. Made sweeter by the man that joined me in it.

We woke early the next morning feeling well-rested, and I knew we couldn't put off leaving. I left Marcus to check us out after breakfast while I walked around the grounds.

I'd just turned a corner when I came to the back of the house and could see this was where the bins were kept. I was just about to turn around when I heard a deep hacking cough, but I could tell by the sound that this came from a child having helped out with enough colds and flu with the children at home. Their coughs sounded different from an adult cough.

Venturing quietly forward to have a look, I heard a whispered conversation.

"Don't worry, Rosie, they'll be throwing out the breakfast soon, and I'll get us something good to eat."

"I don't feel like eating Roman," another child's voice answered, "I'm not feeling good."

"I know, Rosie. I'm sorry."

Hearing a noise behind me, I turned and saw Marcus walking towards me. Putting a finger to my lips, I warned him to keep quiet. He didn't question me, just walked up behind me and wrapped an arm around my waist as I waited. For what, I wasn't certain, but I knew in my heart this was where I was meant to be at this moment.

Not long after, the kitchen doors opened, and one of the staff came out and threw bags into the bin. As soon as the door shut, the body of a small child, I think a boy, ran out from behind the bush. We watched as he quickly pulled the bag open and started rummaging through it, but not before we heard the long hacking cough. I saw his face tense and tears threatening to fall when he heard it, but he continued with his plan of getting them food. Marcus squeezed my hip. I moved forward and said softly, "What are you looking for?"

The child froze, and I could see he wanted to bolt, so I continued.

"If you're hungry, my husband and I can get you something fresh to eat."

The boy turned around, his small face filthy, and long matted dark hair falling in his face. He scowled at me, "I don't need anything from the likes of you," he growled at me, hands clenched.

There was another hacking cough from behind the wall, and another small child stumbled out, also filthy with long dark hair, but her eyes were glazed, and I could see she wasn't well. She was swaying on her feet.

"Roman," she mumbled before she collapsed.

Marcus managed to catch her before she hit the ground.

"Rosie," the little lad cried as he rushed towards his sister. "Let her go, mister. I can look after her."

My heart broke as I watched him try to take his sister from Marcus.

Pulling him back, I held his fighting body in my arms as I shushed him. Exhausted, he finally stopped fighting, and huge sobs wracked his body.

I didn't like the blue tint to Rosie's lips or her laboured breathing. She needed a hospital.

Lifting the boy's head from where it was buried in my shoulder, I held his cheeks between my palms and looked into the most beautiful brown eyes saying firmly, "Roman, you need to listen to me. Are you listening?"

I got a nod.

"Okay, this is what's going to happen. Rosie is very sick and needs a hospital."

I could see the panic in his eyes, "Nooo, they'll separate us."

I shook my head, "Marcus and I are going to do our best to make sure that doesn't happen. Now we need to call for an ambulance and contact our family, who can help. I need you to be brave for Rosie, okay?"

He nodded again before collapsing against me. I hugged him tight and listened to Marcus on the phone calling an ambulance and explaining we'd meet them out front. Picking up Roman, I follow Marcus around to the front of the building.

Once the ambulance was confirmed as coming, he sat on the bench by the bike, pulling a hoodie out of the saddle bags. Marcus wrapped it around the young girl cradled in his arms, his face showing his worry at her condition before he hit another button on his phone.

"Reap, we're going to need you, man. If you're with any of the others, put the call on speaker. That way, everyone can hear."

He then went on to fill them in on the situation.

A week later, we pieced together as much of the children's story as we could. They'd been living on the streets with their mother when she'd been kicked out by her last boyfriend. Somehow, they'd slipped through all the cracks in the system and ended up squatting in a derelict building. Roman said they'd woken up one morning, and their mother had disappeared. They knew enough to be careful on the streets and had found shelter behind the hotel in an old drainage pipe. It had been dry, if not very warm. They'd also been eating food that was thrown out by the hotel.

They'd been alone for about six months when Rosie got sick. She had a bad case of pneumonia, and both children were malnourished and dehydrated.

Marcus and I had known from the beginning that these were our kids. We'd been waiting for them.

We were sitting in a recliner with me snuggled on his lap in a private room in the children's ward, watching over them, when he said, "They're meant to be ours, aren't they beautiful? This is what you've been waiting for."

I tilted my head back on his shoulder so I could see his face before replying, "Yeah, honey, these kids are ours."

He nodded, "Okay then," he said, letting his head fall back against the chair and closing his eyes.

Two years later, they were finally ours with our name. Maggie and Dog had stepped forward as temporary foster parents again, so we'd got to keep them with us from the beginning. It wasn't all sweetness and light; both children had to learn to trust again. It took Roman longer than Rosie, but nearly a year to the day we'd found them, he called Rogue 'Dad' when they were playing cricket with the others. I thought my man was going to cry.

I certainly did.

We still travelled, but now we went in a campervan and camped instead. Marcus and I went by ourselves for a long weekend on the bike twice a year. One was always on our anniversary. The other was any weekend the children chose for us.

I truly felt blessed and couldn't believe the change in my life after meeting my Rogue on Bournemouth beach.

THE END!

A BIT OF INFO ON PCOS AND ENDOMETRIOSIS

PCOS is one of the most common endocrine disorders in women of reproductive age and one of the biggest causes of infertility. It is thought to affect about 1 in every 10 women in the UK.

There are three main features to PCOS and they are: - irregular periods – which means your ovaries do not regularly release eggs (ovulation). Excess androgen – high levels of "male" hormones in your body, which may cause physical signs such as excess facial or body hair. Polycystic ovaries – your ovaries become enlarged and contain many fluid-filled sacs (follicles) that surround the eggs.

But you can also have all or some of the following, They can include: weight gain, thinning hair and hair loss from the head, oily skin or acne.

The cause of PCOS is unknown, but it often runs in families (it does in mine). There is no cure for PCOS however symptoms can be treated.

Endometriosis - is a condition where tissue similar to the lining of the womb grows in other places, such as the ovaries and fallopian tubes. Endometriosis can affect women of any age, including teenagers. It's a long-term condition that can have a significant impact on your life.

You can have the two conditions together.

Acknowledgements

I would like to say a massive thank you to my Beta Readers Cloe Rowe and Clare. F. you ladies rock.

To my husband for always encouraging me on whatever crazy idea takes me at the time. Being there for me, always putting me first and for treating me like a queen. After 27 years you are still my inspiration.

My eldest daughter Helen offered positive quotes and comments daily during this journey. I love you more than the whole world and don't know what I would do without you and your encouragement. Love you, baby.

To my youngest, my lovely Ria, I love your snarky comments when we have to share the same space while I write. Don't ever change. Love you to the moon and back.

To my mum who keeps our house running smoothly, I honestly don't know what I would do without you. Love you.

To all my readers who took a chance on me with my first book Wild & Free and for reaching out with positive comments and suggestions.

One last thing .... **REVIEWS** feed an author's soul, and we learn and grow from them. Whether it be just a rating left or a few words they are what pushes us to keep writing.

About the Author

I grew up on a cattle farm on the outskirts of a small town in Zambia, Southern Central Africa. I went to school in South Africa, Zambia and finally finished my schooling in Zimbabwe. I had an amazing childhood filled with fantastic experiences. As a family, we often went on holiday to Lake Kariba and I feel very privileged to have seen Victoria Falls, one of the seven wonders of the world several times.

My grandparents lived on the same farm as my parents and me. It was my grandmother, my Ouma who first introduced me to the romance genre by passing her Mills and Boons on to me, and I was hooked from there.

I now live happily in Jane Austen country in the UK with my family, VA by day and wordsmith by night.

Follow me:

https://www.facebook.com/michelle.dups.5/

https://www.instagram.com/author_michelle_dups

www.michelledups.carrd.co

https://www.goodreads.com/michelledups

https://www.facebook.com/groups/837078130666476

Other Books by Author

Sanctuary Series

Sanctuary Book 1 – Wild and Free (Dex & Reggie)

Sanctuary Book 2 - Angel (Kyle & Lottie)

Sanctuary Book 3 – Julie (Julie & Joel)

Sanctuary Book 4 – Amy a Novella (Amy, Sean and Rory) Amy won't be coming out as a paperback due to its size. Instead, it will be as an extra in the back of Julie.

Sanctuary Book 5 – The Russos (coming soon)

Sanctuary Book 6 - 2024

Crow MC

Reaper

Onyx

Rogue

Draco – Summer 23

Dragon – TBA

Avy – TBA

Noni - TBA

Navy - TBA